T0194053

Truly

Truly

D.E. Payne

iUniverse®

TRULY

iUniverse books may be ordered through booksellers or by contacting:

iUniverse
1663 Liberty Drive
Bloomington, IN 47403
www.iuniverse.com
1-800-Authors (1-800-288-4677)

ISBN: 978-1-5320-7001-3 (sc)
ISBN: 978-1-5320-7003-7 (hc)
ISBN: 978-1-5320-7002-0 (e)

Print information available on the last page.

iUniverse rev. date: 04/01/2019

Contents

I lovingly dedicate this book to my sister, Christine White, (1960 - 2016), a writer herself, who encouraged me to write this novel.

1

In The Beginning

The gently tinkling of the small brass bell over the door startles the old book store owner out of his daze and before he even looks, he knows it's her. As the day grew late, with a feeling of sadness, he thought by double checking his wall calendar, still he had all but given up hope until this very moment. She has come to his 'Olde Book Shoppe' for the last four years on this very same day, today being the fifth year. She is a pretty young thing, maybe in her mid thirties, quiet, nicely dressed. She always smiles and nods at him, then goes straight to the Romantic Fantasy section and slowly browses every book on the shelf. Whenever he's gone over to offer assistance, she gently turns and smiling says "thank you but it will come to me if it's here." What does that mean, he wonders, 'it will come to me.' He settles back to watch her, still fascinated after all these years.

Mesmerized by her small hand as it glides over the books, touching each one in turn, he notices a beautiful diamond and sapphire rings on her right hand, next to that is a circle of diamonds and a flat white gold band. This makes him wonder what's on her left hand when suddenly, she raises that hand to steady herself. On the ring finger of her left hand is a beautiful large, multi diamond ring, on the inside of that is a circle of diamonds set in yellow gold, followed by two, very original, antique wedding bands. How uniquely interesting. On the middle finger of her left hand is a large oval sapphire surrounded by diamonds, just beautiful.

Suddenly, one book stops her, seemingly to jump right off the shelf, coming to life in her hands. She is smiling now, her eyes glistening. Taking the book with her, she settles into one of the upholstered love seats the old gentleman has provided for his patrons. As she makes herself comfortable to read, the old man settles in to watch her.

Time has no meaning for each of them now it seems. After an hour, the chill snaps him awake. Moving quietly he turns up the heat then decides to put the tea kettle on. Passing the front door, he sees that it's now dark outside. Checking his watch, he flips the closed sign over, then goes into his little kitchen. Carrying two tea cups, he quietly places one in front of the lady who absently reaches for it, smiling her thanks up to him. He never noticed before but she has the most beautiful blue eyes.

Taking his cup back to his desk, he once again perches on his stool. He knows he'll sit here all night if the lady wants to read. Smiling to himself, he doesn't exactly knows why.

Almost five hours later, he glances up as she slowly closes the book. Not wanting this special time, or the story to end, studying the book cover, she sees the few lines there but doesn't read them, instead, she looks to the bottom where the name of the author is printed. Smiling, she gathers up her coat and bag then handing the book to the old man on her way past, she smiles and quietly says "thank you for your kindness" before walking through the door. Standing up as she passes, curious now, he watches as she walks across the road into the darkness. On the other side, patiently waiting for her are four very tall, good looking gentlemen, all wearing blue tunics and high black boots, silver swords hang from their belts. The ghost of six large, majestic horses stand behind them. A slightly older lady is waiting with the men, she's wearing a long blue dress and now, as he looks back to the younger lady, she is also wearing a long, blue dress. Those waiting for her all have loving smiles on their faces and he's sure the lady's face is reflective of theirs. As she reaches them, they part and she takes her place between two of the men, linking arms together, they continue their walk into the park, then suddenly disappear.

The old man stands there for a moment, trying to re-visualize what he just saw but knowing deep in his heart that it is true. Looking at the book in his hand, he reads the author's name - Princess Dawn Elizabeth. Looking up at the now empty park in front of him, he smiles. Going back to his desk to finally pack up and go home for the night, he tucks the book into his bag.

2

First Date ... Let the Adventure Begin

Where do I begin to tell this love story. It didn't start out that way. Firstly, let me introduce my self. My Name is Dawn Elizabeth. I have lived and worked in St. Pete's, California for the past three years. The city is very exciting and I fit in well, fast paced, high energy, lots of great photo ops. Photography is my passion, getting a job in an architectural firm was a bonus. Seeing the awesome scenery and building plans 'in the making' is just another notch in my artistic belt. Not that I'm doing any designing or anything like that but working alongside people who are gives me a glimpse of the work in motion, enough so to keep me inspired and moving forward with my hobbies. Yes, hobbies. I'm sure you heard that breaking into Hollywood is hard, well St. Pete's is sooo full of talented artists of every type, that getting noticed is almost impossible ... unless you know someone.

Well, I personally didn't know anyone but my boss does. His name is Rick. He started this firm ten years ago in Canada with a partner who left to pursue a modeling career. Rick moved the business here to California where he is now doing famously well, designing homes for the stars and beginning to expand all over the world.

Anyways, I remember it well, it was a beautiful Tuesday morning and things were going unusually smooth at the office when I looked up from my desk to see a gorgeous man sitting on the corner of Rick's desk, laughing with him, seeming very at ease. I wonder if this could be the lost partner. Caught staring, I think my heart actually leapt out of my chest. Quickly standing up, I almost trip in my haste to move around my desk and head for the ladies room, severe anxiety attack... Elizabeth, a co-worker and good friend, appears in the doorway wondering what the heck is wrong with me. "Ready for lunch" she asks. "What???" Oh, running back to my desk to get my purse, I notice that Rick and the stranger are gone. Am I disappointed?

When Rick gets back from an extended lunch, he has a mysterious smile on his face. Watching him through the glass partition wall of his office, I'm guessing he is mentally going over his lunchtime conversation as, at times, he actually laughs out loud to himself.

As I'm packing up to leave at 5:00, he saunters out of his office and perches on the corner of my desk, not saying anything.

Getting that gut-wrenching feeling in the pit of my stomach, he smiles and says "that guy you saw in my office earlier is my silent partner, he's been my best friend for the past 20 years, we went through University together and started this business. We try to get together as often as we can which is not often enough." Laughing to himself, Rick goes on "he's a great guy and I really like and respect him."

'OK' I'm thinking to myself. "Anyways" Rick smiles at me now, "he asked about you, said he would like to meet you and maybe ask you out." Gulp! Why are my hands shaking? My face must have gone white because Rick just smiles. "So, what should I tell him?" "Well, I don't know. He looks interesting but I don't know him." Meanwhile, my mind is saying something totally different like 'wow, this guy is hot and smart and he's interested in me.' While my mind is racing madly, I must have been pulling faces and squinting my eyes because I caught myself when I heard Rick laughing his head off. OK, I'm back. "Listen Dawn, I know you and I know Jacob, I can see why he's attracted to you and I think you'll like him. Go for it. I'll tell him to give you a call when he's in town, next week I think."

Later in the week, every time my phone rings at work or at home, I start to hyperventilate. Ends up, he didn't call at all, he came into the office a week later and Rick wasn't in, I didn't know what to do, where to look. Sauntering into Rick's office, he looks around then spies me. As he walks over, he has that soft smile on his face, almost making you wonder what he's up to and with a sparkle in his warm, brown eyes. He is sweet. I can say this now, at the time, I could not breath or think, my hands were clammy. I really don't remember what I stammered.

I do remember that first date. He was a perfect gentleman, nicely dressed in casual slacks and an open neck, long sleeved shirt, longish hair but tied back neatly and very clean. We walked to a very nice Italian restaurant close to the office and sat on the outside, covered patio. He didn't want to scare me off by getting in his car. I thought that was very considerate of him. He suggested a bottle of red wine as he hoped I would stay for a meal. When I hesitated and reminded him it was Thursday and I had work tomorrow, he just smiled and pulled out his cell. Casually punching in a few buttons, mumbling two or three words only, he flipped the phone closed and said "no work tomorrow" with a big grin on his face. What!! He had called Rick and told him we were on our "first" date and Rick was so thrilled and laughing, he said "tell Dawn she has the day off tomorrow... with pay." Holy cow, talk about having the support of your boss on a date. Wow!

Well, I couldn't keep the smile off my face, all the while already starting to worry what would happen if this ended badly, Jacob being friends with my boss and all. Anyways, that was a quick flash in the pan of my mind, I couldn't worry for long, looking into the smiling face across the bistro table from me, the setting sun leaving a red tint across the street and buildings.

Laughing... I wished I had my camera with me. Click... a picture in my mind.

The evening went by amazingly fast. We enjoyed the wine, of course, I felt it with the first sip, then my head started to even out to a nice, little buzz, I didn't want to miss a moment of this. When it cooled down outside, the owner personally came out and invited us in, placing us in a cozy corner table with a curved leather upholstered seat, so we were now sitting side by side. After two hours of conversation, laughing and sharing, we were very comfortable with each other when he took my hand in his and held it.

I was happy to let him do the ordering, he knows his Italian, I ate so much, no room for dessert.

I didn't want the evening to end, neither did he. The restaurant was now full with a line up waiting so it was time to go.

On the street, we headed to a red Mustang, older model I think, roof down. Smiling, he asks "like to go for a ride, maybe see the bridge with the lights on." The cafes that sit along the waterfront as well as the boats on the water were ablaze with tiny, white lights. What a picture this would make but in my mind only as my camera was at home. Maybe next time ...

We ended up heading north towards Mara, driving along the narrow highway that hugs the coast. Some areas on the water were black and scary for me but the sky was full of stars, with the cool breeze blowing through my hair, I wasn't concerned with anything. Jacob had asked me what I wanted to do, adding that he had a home in the Mara hills. If I felt safe with him, we could go back there, have a drink and watch the stars or take a dip in the pool. It was already 1:00 am. Neither of us wanted the evening to end and he assured me 'no pressure, no funny stuff, I was in charge...' and I believed him and trusted him.

His home was beautiful, all glass and wood made from local Mara stone, blending into the earth, at one with nature, kind of like him. Nice. He told me he designed the house, wanting an open concept, lots of windows to let in the light but with large overhangs to shield the inside from too much sun or heat. Very modern, every convenience made to measure. The back yard faces the city of Mara and the ocean so there is always a wonderful view, a nice breeze and privacy. Because of the climate, the gardens around the house comprise of local rock, sand and desert type plants. The whole back of the house is glass with doors emerging from various rooms at various levels, the kitchen, the living room, walking you out onto large cedar wood decks that stay cool even under the hot sun.

Most of the back yard is a large pool with wide steps leading down into a deeper end. At the far corner is a small waterfall that you could actually sit under. Very nice. A corner rock area includes a small pond for local frogs, salamanders and small lizards that like to hang there. On the deck outside of the kitchen, a patio table with lounge chairs sit under a large umbrella, also on the deck is an oversized, brick grill.

Of course, I couldn't see all of this until the next morning when, wearing one of Jacobs' shirts, I'm looking out the bedroom window. Still in bed, leaning up on one elbow watching me, he gives me one of his sweet smiles.

When we arrived at his place, he showed me around in the dark. There were outside lights all over the grounds and the moon was shining brightly down on us. Inside, he lit candles that seemed to be everywhere. It was bright enough to see without any problem and the candles added a nice romantic glow. He swears this wasn't planned. "Oh yeah," I tell him, laughing. "He probably does this for all his dates..." He almost, almost seems hurt, then he laughs quietly, thoughtfully. Mmmmm.

White wine now, I'm getting my second wind, feeling good and craving something sweet. When he opens the refrigerator, I see dark, rich brownies and chocolate chip cookies, they look home made. Catching me eyeing the treats, he pulls a container of vanilla ice cream out of the freezer. We make ourselves bowls of chocolate brownies and ice cream. Add a bottle of chilled white wine and laying on lounge chairs outside under the stars, you have a perfect night.

I think I actually saw the sky start to lighten up but by now my eyes are closing, so are his. Standing up, taking my hand he leads me inside and up to the bedroom. Stripping down to his boxers, he hands me a fresh t-shirt, while he's in the bathroom, I undress and slip into bed. Smelling the shirt, it would be nice to have his fragrance on me. Laying down under the covers, almost asleep now, I feel him move in behind me, pulling the covers up over both of us. Putting his arm around me, he kisses my cheek.

D.E. Payne

The next thing I hear is the chirping of birds outside the bedroom window. Rubbing my eyes, I roll out of bed and walk over to the window. The full sun is shining high in the sky, blinding me. What time is it anyways and what happened last night. I know what I remember but...

Turning, I see Jacob rubbing his eyes and laughing, shaking his head. I can't help but start to laugh as well. We slept together and he hasn't even kissed me yet. Climbing back into bed, I snuggle up, giving him a nice, gentle kiss on the lips. Looking me in the eyes for a second he smiles... then starts kissing me back.

3

3 Months Later - Home to Stay

I didn't see much of Jacob during the next few months, he often worked 20 hours a day, five, maybe six days straight. Sometimes, he'd call me at the office to say he missed me and we'd make plans to get together. Other times I'd get a call late at night when I was already in bed and he was still at work. Of course, when I didn't hear from him for a day or two, I'd think he had changed his mind and that was that, silly me. I filled my time with Elizabeth, my friend from work, we would go for drives, take pictures, thinking of Jacob. He was always anxious to see my photos and hear about what I'd done while he was away. Good news is, Rick really likes me and although he rarely speaks to Jacob without me knowing, he always confirms Jacob's feelings for me, he is thrilled with our relationship.

Jacob is actually coming up to a long weekend off, hard to believe but true. During the last three months, we saw each other as often as we could but because of his long days and irregular schedule, time together consisted of dinner together, a drive along the coast, walks on the beach, never more than one day at a time so basically, we are just dating.

Finally three full days and nights off work but would they be three days together for us? Would Jacob have some other plans for a day or two, would he even want to spend that long with me? Stopping my mind from running away with itself, I know he's having a difficult time of this, as much or more so than me from some things he says, interesting ...

Saying he would be at my apartment at 7:00 Friday night, I have time to go home, shower and make myself pretty for him with a few extra minutes to straighten up. Packing a small overnight bag, I grab my cameras, you never know when a great photo op will present itself. I'm more inspired and in artists eye mode as Jacob really seems interested and likes my photos.

The ringing of the doorbell announces his arrival, I'm feeling very nervous. "Hi babe" he says leaning down to give me a kiss. Sitting in my only armchair, there's that smile again and there goes my heart, I'm sure he can hear it.

Indicating for me to have a seat on the sofa, he gets down on both knees so we're eye to eye, smiling, he holds up a small, blue box.

"I bought something for you, something special and beautiful so you know how much I care about you" he chokes out and opening the box, he holds up a beautiful sapphire ring surrounded by diamonds. Taking the ring from him with shaking hands, my eyes start to blur with the beginning of tears, as I try to blink them away, one falls onto the ring. Taking my hand, he kisses the ring and places it on the ring finger of my left hand, he has tears in his eyes now as well. "I'm falling in love with you" he says, "you know how I feel about marriage but I want to show you how I feel about you" he adds and now we're both laughing. Swinging me up in his arms, we dance around my small living room. "Let's go."

With my overnight bag in one hand and my camera bag over his shoulder, we leave my apartment and jump into his red convertible. "I want to take you to meet my parents on Sunday, we'll spend the day, probably go out to dinner with them, they know I'm coming and am bringing someone special" he says, his brows going up like an evil man in a horror show. Oh oh, parents, both university professors. "What if they don't like me?" I ask, already worried. "Don't worry, they'll love you" he laughs.

The drive along the winding coast to Mara is delightful, the warm breeze blowing in our hair, the sun sinking over the ocean.

I feel comfortable in his home and finally, I'm going to meet Matilda, Mattie he calls her, Jacob's housekeeper, the live in lady who takes care of him. Their families have known each other for years he tells me, she's a great cook and baker and she loves him like a Mother.

He's good to her and she to him, she also seems to know about me and already likes me. Thank you kind lady.

The evening air is still quite warm and after a day at the office, a nice swim is just the thing. Changing into a one-piece bathing suit, I come downstairs from the upper level and find a lovely dinner has been laid out on the patio table, complete with white napkins, white wine, vanilla candles and a small, silver bowl filled with white baby roses. Wow! How romantic. Admiring my new ring, I catch Mattie's smile and quickly turn away. It's beautiful, I'm overwhelmed and it fits perfectly. Mmmmm ...

After cooling off in the pool, over dinner, Jacob is sitting beside me looking very happy but nervous, anxious. "There's something I want to ask you" he says very slowly, I can almost feel his mind racing. "I know it may seem kind of soon but ... I'd love you to move in here with me, I'm off for the next three months." Taking a breath, he continues "not being able to see you these past few months has made me crazy and also made me realize something. I want you, I need you. It's taken me a long time to soften my heart and now that I have, I know you're the one that I want" (hey, isn't that a song or something).

I can't speak, I'm stunned, wildly happy but stunned. As I sit there with my mouth hanging open, Jacob takes me in his arms and kisses me, really kisses me. My smile probably gives him my answer without me saying a word ... and then he leads me up to the bedroom.

We make love, slow, tender, loving love, we are one with each other, nothing else matters, no one else exists. This is the way it should be, the only way and now I have my answer, now I know. Yes, I would be moving in with him.

4

Meeting Sam & Lil' J

How can anyone sleep with the sun shining in on us, the sky is a beautiful blue, the view spectacular. I'm up, showered, have a perfect cup of tea in front of me and am downloading the photos I took yesterday. Walking out of the bathroom, wet hair and with a towel wrapped around his waist, Jacob walks over to where I'm sitting and kneeling down to look at my computer screen says "beautiful, just beautiful, oh and your photos are as well" he laughs. "You know, I knew when I designed this desk in front of the window, it was for someone and something very special. I can design a custom office for you, however you like." He's grinning ear to ear.

His warm, clean smell just makes me want to kiss his face all over. Ah, there's that soft, warm smile again. To put an end to his misery, although I'm truly enjoying this, I just say "yes, ok, ok" shrugging my shoulders like I hate to give in, trying not to break into a smile. "I love you and would like to live here with you." Jumping up he lets out a woop that actually scares me to almost falling off the chair then he grabs me under my arms and swings me around the room. Ow, ok put me down, laughing, both of us fall onto the bed. Laying there, crossways, I ask "how is this going to work? My office is an hour away." "Oh that, I have that all figured out. Let's grab a cup of tea and go outside and I can tell you all about it. I've already talked to Rick ..."

Sitting at the patio table with a whole spread of breakfast foods in front of us, fruit, yogurt, mini, bite size pancakes and Mattie's homemade fruit Danish, Jacob starts to lay out his and Rick's plans. "When did you do all this, talk to Rick? He's been out of town for a week." I ask Jacob who just chuckles. "Rick and I had this all planned out weeks ago." WEEKS AGO..!

Rick had been planning on moving the office to Mara for some time now. With him flying to his customers all over the US, it's mostly the design work that's done in the office, as well as my pricing and bookkeeping stuff and both of these things can be done anywhere. Rick is originally from Mara so was thrilled at the prospect of moving back and Jacob will probably have a hand in some designing as well, a bonus for both men. Jacob has already been working on the designs for a new house for Rick and his family in the hills. This would be great for me, so great, I could continue doing a job I love for a real nice boss. I'm sure Rick is thrilled as well. Those sneaky beggars.

I am so excited I decide to let everything just sink in, digest it slowly, enjoy every treasured moment of it.

We are planning on going into Mara for supper and I can't wait to get some nice pics at night with all the lights on in town. Mara is a small, old, Spanish style town, very colourful, a photographers paradise. What a lovely place to live. I am, well, we are very blessed.

The best laid plans of mice and men ... Hanging up his cell, Jacob tells me Sam, an old friend who lives near here would like to come for a swim. "Are we still going into town?" I ask.

Ring ... ring... JACOB! JACOB! "Hi Lil' fellow, how's my big boy?" says 'Big' Jacob as he scoops up the Lil' boy and swings him around the foyer. Yelling and screaming continue from both the boys as 'Big' Jacob throws the boy high in the air before easily catching him. His mother, Samantha slides in the front door as I'm watching the scene, not sure if they realize I'm here. Kneeling down on the floor, speaking quietly to Lil' Jacob, Jacob says "hey Lil' J, I have someone I want you to meet, a special lady. Someone I really like and I know you'll like her too, ok? Are you ready?" "Where is she? I never saw any special lady here before, is she hiding?" "No, she's right here so come on". Meeting at the bottom of the stairs, Jacob says "this is Donna, Donna, this is Lil' J."

When I hear his name, my brows go up and I shoot Jacob a quick look. He has already read my thoughts and is laughing and shaking his head no. "Hi Jacob, it's nice to meet you" I say to the Lil' blond. "Hi, are you coming swimming with us?" "No, I don't think so" I answer seeing Jacob shaking his head. Seeming to know his way around, Lil' J runs out into the back yard as Sam yells not to go near the water. As Jacob and Sam embrace she tentatively glances my way then a smile breaks out on her face. "It's about time" she laughs to Jacob. In answer to my questioning look, she says "I knew Jacob was up to something then I finally got it out of him, it's really nice to finally meet you" Sam smiles. Jacob smiles. I smile.

Hearing squeals of delight, we all run outside and find Lil' J in the corner pond, holding a very green frog. "Look, look" he yells to all of us in general, me included, I guess I've been accepted. Grabbing my camera I snap a few pics of Lil' J holding up the frog to show me. Noticing Sam and Jacob standing at the top of the stairs, whispering together, I continue taking pictures including one of Sam, Lil' J and the frog together. The photo is priceless. Sam is smiling up at me, Lil' J has his mouth open and is looking at the frog as it jumps out of his hands. Perfect. Big J rescues the frog before it ends up in the swimming pool and returns it to the pond, telling Lil' J to leave it alone now. Stripping off his outer clothing to reveal his swimming trunks underneath, Lil' J yells "let's go mom."

Jacob is telling Sam of our plans to hit the beach, shop for clothes to "meet the parents" and have a nice supper at one of the many restaurants in town when Mattie brings out a tray of tall, cool drinks for all of us, she seems to already know Sam and Lil' J.

At the pools edge, Lil' J has his water wings on and is splashing in the shallow water while inside we can see Mattie organizing plates of food. Jacob excuses himself and heads inside as Sam turns and smiles at me. "I know you probably have questions about Jacob and my relationship so I want to set you straight right off." Smiling at the memories she is about to share with me she goes on "I've known and worked with Jacob for about 6 years. When you work day and night with people, you become family. I was in a relationship, albeit a short one, a few years ago with what I thought was an ok guy. My clock was ticking and I really wanted to have a child before it was too late. I got pregnant quickly and everything between us seemed to be going along fine. The guy was in on this plan but....

Soon after my son was born, he bolted and I mean bolted. For almost a year, I had no idea where he even was. Naturally, I was freaking until Jacob came to my rescue. I called him one night shortly after Lil' Jacob's father took off and he came right over, he's been there for us ever since. Lil' J's real, christened name is not really Jacob but we soon started calling him that because he seemed to think it was his name." My heart tells me it is so, Jacob is thrilled and proud and Lil' J absolutely loves Jacob. Samantha continues "he has, in his childish way, asked me if Jacob is his dad and I have explained it to him. Jacob has been more to me and Lil' J than he even knows. I hope you're ok with this."

Well, I have to sit and digest this for a minute, my heart is aching for the special bond that Sam and Jacob have but then the smart side of my brain tells me that

Jacob loves me. Of course, all these thoughts happen at lightening speed and the next thing Sam is saying is that she feels her and I will become great friends, she can feel it.... and so can I. I've just met this woman but feel that she would never betray me.

When Jacob comes back, conveniently timed I might add, he's smiling. I think this time with Sam was his plan. Smart man I have here. Reaching out his hand, he asks "are you ready to go and don't forget your camera." A glance at Sam, a turn of his hand action and a nod tells me that Sam has her own key and will lock up when they leave. Ok then ...

5

Jacob & I Shop and Dine in Mara

On the drive down the mountain, Jacob points out where all the movie stars live like he's giving me a tour, laughing all the way because he's not impressed by 'movie stars' ... but I am! Mara is a beautiful, colourful, Spanish town set at the ocean's door. The locals really appreciate and celebrate the traditions, having come from humble ancestry, you can see and hear this when you talk to them. On the other side, with all the high class, very expensive stores that cater to the tourists and the local celebrities, it's an amazing town where you can find every single thing that you might wish for... and more. I love it ... and the photo opportunities.

The smell of bbq beef is waffling through the air, pulling us in the direction of a fancy looking restaurant. The sun is setting as twinkling lights around the city come on. "Do you feel like roast beef?" he asks me. Do I ever, just smelling that and now I'm starving, it is 6:00.

"A nice, cosy corner, maybe by the window with a view of the ocean but without the cool breeze" the maitre'd suggests, smiling. 'Sounds perfect to me.' The chairs are red velvet, very dark as are the heavy drapes that hang on the floor to ceiling windows. Very romantic. A fragrant rose candle burns in the centre of the table and heavy silver cutlery is set on a white linen tablecloth. My menu doesn't have any prices on it and Jacob laughs, saying "order anything you want."

The waiter is surprised that I know Yorkshire pudding. I tell him I'm from Canada and know where to find the best roast beef and Yorkshire. After he walks away, a surprised Jacob says "I didn't know you were Canadian, I don't think Rick does either. Another special thing about you, I knew it was something but never would have guessed that one." So while I'm into surprising him, I say "did you know that I'm also a Christian"? Reaching across to take my hand, he says "again, I knew you were special and now it's all coming together."

Suddenly, another man is standing at our table holding a nice, chilled bottle of white African wine I know from Canada. Apparently, the waiter had gone to the owner and told him Jacob was here with a friend from Canada. The owner, a friend of Jacob's, is thrilled to see him ... and meet me. Yeah! A beautiful bottle of complimentary wine from a very happy restaurateur. I did see him eyeing my ring and laughing, Jacob caught that as well. Celebrate good times I say. The meal was spectacular, just delicious, perfect in every way ... and no room for dessert.

We were both feeling pretty good when we walked out of that restaurant and so was the owner, his tables were full to capacity, people tend to follow me.

6

I Don't Want to go

I'm rarely in this bad of a mood. Walking downstairs to get myself a coffee, I realize part of what is worrying me right now is I have been so happy these past few days and now ... I don't think I can handle going back to my old life, not after having this and by this, I mean Jacob. You do have Jacob, nothing has changed, face it, you simply don't want to leave here, even if it's only to pack up your apartment, your previous 2 ½ years that you forged out for yourself. That's what happens when you move on to something better, you can never go back.

Sitting with my coffee on the deck steps, bum sitting three stairs up from where my feet are drumming, I hear Jacob quietly come up behind me, a coffee in his hands. He knows me well enough already, maybe more than I know myself. How can that be in so short a time? Maybe

I'm more transparent than I intend to be, is that good or bad.

He doesn't say a word but sits on the step beside me, a questioning look in his eyes, I can't even look at him, I feel like such a baby as tears sting my eyes. Laughing his soft, all knowing quiet laugh, he puts his arm around my shoulders saying "I know, this is hard, it's ok, I love you, this will be great, I promise you." OK, that helps. Trying to smile through blurry eyes I see the sun trying to break through, the clouds seem a little whiter now.

"I don't want to leave you, leave here, I don't want to go back to my apartment, back to work, I just don't want to go" I wail, wrapping my arms tightly around him. "And I don't want you to leave" he tells me. "Let me make a call, ok, be right back." Following him into the kitchen, he picks up his cell and hits a button. Instantly, someone at the other end picks up. "Hi, I'm great, she's great as well, oh really great" a raunchy laugh between guys. "She's the reason I'm calling, no, I'm not sick of her yet" he glances at me and laughs. I can hear Rick laughing at the other end, it's nice to be with people who like you.

"Yup, ok, ok. Ok, talk to you later. Call me back at this number, we'll be in Palm Springs by then, bye for now, here she is" and he hands me the phone. "Hi!" Rick just wanted to confirm what he had said to Jacob so I wouldn't start to give him the third degree. Rick is going to be out of the country till Thursday, Elizabeth can handle the office this week. She'll put anything I need to take care of through to the house number, not to worry, everything's good. When I hang up the cell with Rick, Jacob is just hanging up the house phone.

"Grab a coffee and lets plan this out ok" he smiles. Settled in on the patio, he hesitates for a moment to think, then says "we can do this a few different ways. What do you have at your apartment that you want to keep?" Well, that gets me thinking. "Actually, almost everything there I bought when I moved in so nothing has any real sentimental meaning to me. I have a few things I want, nothing big though" I answer him. "Ok, that's a good start, I can send in movers to pack up your place and bring it here, along with your car or we can take a drive down, you can say goodbye, pick up the stuff you want and..." "Oh, I know" I interrupt, "Mama Lee's daughter, who lives downstairs with her parents and young son could probably use most everything I have. She moved downstairs so they could rent out the apartment to pay her way through University. Her parents, grandfather, herself and her son are all crammed into one small house. Wouldn't it be nice if they could open up the house again, she could live upstairs, finish her schooling."

Jacob is listening to my thinking out loud without saying a word. "Done." What? "OK, why don't we do that. Let's take a drive down. You can pick up what you want, give the apartment back to the Lees', fully furnished. They'll be happy, you'll be doing a very good thing and we won't have to pack up and move anything" he smiles. "And I'll give them a cheque to cover any loss of rent and for Sing Lee to finish her schooling. Everybody's happy, right baby, will that work for you?"

Mad little knocking at the front door informs us Lil J has arrived. Sam is just pulling the booster seat out of her Mustang and carrying it over to the garage door, she also has three large plastic tubs with lids. "For your stuff" she smiles at me, "are you ok with us coming along" she asks.

The garage door opens and I hear the roar of a powerful engine. I've actually never seen the door open or the inside of the two car garage. Jacob's at the wheel of a bright yellow vehicle, gigantic.

Pulling out of the garage, he turns it off, jumps out and starts to put the booster seat inside behind the driver. Struggling, Sam steps in to take it from him and laughing he throws up his arms and walks over to get the bins.

The inside of the vehicle is huge, Sam, Lil J and I look like tiny people sitting there, only Jacob looks the right size. It's nice sitting so high, you can see over the cars in front of you and have a good view of the ocean. Oh no, I forgot my big camera but I do have my purse size one in my bag, I can't believe I walked out of the house without it, too much on my mind I guess. I do have my apartment key though, like I'm going to need it, I called ahead and spoke to Sing Lee, they'll be waiting for us.

The front door swings open as we climb out of the car, Sing Lee is waiting, smiling at us all. Introductions are made all around before we all troop upstairs to my small, bachelor apartment, Sing Lee and her young son following us up. She was very excited when I told her of my, er ... Jacob's plans.

Not really expecting the emotions I'm now feeling, I walk around, looking out the windows at the beautiful gardens that surround the house, meanwhile Jacob has brought up the plastic bins and set them out around the room. Looking closely at each item to decide if I really want or need to keep it, I finally decided to take only my personal stuff, clothes, paints and brushes, of course, all my camera stuff and my stuffed animals. Lil J has his eye on them so I thought I would take them now and give his some later. Asking Sing Lee's son if there's anything special he might like, he happily picks out one or two of his favourites. I'm basically leaving Sing Lee a fully furnished apartment and she could not have been more grateful or gracious. Watching as Jacob quietly takes her aside, he speaks privately to her before handing her a cheque. Unfolding it, she gasps, her eyes watering before running downstairs to her mother, her son doesn't understand why his mother is crying and runs after her, starting to cry as well. We are in their prayers for life as well as in their family story, probably for generations to come. Kind of humbles you, I'll miss this family.

Everyone helps pack and we're done in no time. As Jacob is carrying bins out to the car, Mama Lee puts a hand on his arm and leads him into their living room. Sing Lee is standing there as well as Grandfather, Mama Lee bows low over and over again, speaking quickly in Chinese. Jacob doesn't know where to look or what to say. Sing Lee translates and tells him, in detail, how his kind generosity would be used and the end result this would make to a family he does not even know. Gulp. Smiles all around as Sam and I come downstairs and stand in the living room behind Jacob.

The two boys are now playing together in the next room and Grandfather has presented Jacob with a beautifully embellished red and gold key ring with long tassels on it and attached is a special key to their home.

The symbolism of this is that Jacob will always be a welcome guest not only in their home but in the home of every family member. This word of gentle generosity will be spread more quickly that we can ever imagine. As we pick up the bins, preparing to leave, Sing Lee quickly calls us back into the dining room where the table is set, full of home made, original Chinese food. We are invited to stay for lunch, ok, we could eat.

Sitting around the table, in proper Chinese tradition, the eldest goes first. We watch as Grandfather then Mama Lee fill their bowls then we each followed suit. Sam, Jacob and I smile at each other not wanting to be the next to follow, an age thing. Anyways, the food is unbelievable.

Hugs, kisses and prayerful bows later, we slam the car doors shut, buckle our seat belts and am finally on our way. What an experience. As Jacob pulls the car away from the house, he pats a brown paper bag sitting between our seats. "Doggie bag" he smiles. Looking back at the house as we drive away ... hey, my car is already gone ...

The drive home is quiet, each of us deep in our thoughts, good, nice thoughts. I will truly miss this family and will keep in touch. I imagine their son, Tom, who works for Rick's firm, will be moving to Mara with his family, so that will be nice.

Parking in our driveway, Sam carries a sleeping Lil J out of his bumper sear and heads straight to her Mustang as Jacob carries the car seat over, he still can't figure out how to install it. "He's exhausted" Sam says, "me too." Grabbing a little stuffed dog I saw Lil J eyeing, I tuck it under his arm as Sam hugs me saying "thanks for a great day, awesome." Giving Jacob a hug goodbye, she drives off. "Let's just leave the bins in the car for tonight, we can get them tomorrow." It's dark outside now and Jacob happily agrees but grabs the doggie bag.

Worn out but happy, Jacob takes the bags into the kitchen and starts to rip them open. "Are you hungry again?" I ask, laughing. Picking up the food and some bowls, he heads for the living room, a room I've never been in. "Honey, why don't you grab that white wine in the fridge and some glasses." OK! By the time I step into the room, he's sitting on the floor, the bags are open. There are no chairs but large, black, beanbag type cushions, very comfortable and surprisingly easy to sit in. Handing him the wine and glasses, I sit down crossed legged on the floor and noticing one bag unopened, emptying the contents on the table, it's fortune cookies with home made written messages.

I've done this before at the Lee's. As Jacob watches me, I hold my hand over each cookie then select one. "You do the same, one will be drawn to you, the other two are for Sam and Lil J. You won't believe how true these fortunes will be. Save it for after we eat and don't tell me what your fortune says, hide it in your underwear drawer or something." He laughs as I raise my eyebrows ... and what is this ... chop sticks ...

7

Deliver the goods

Waking up early the next morning, I feel pretty good, the sun is shining brightly through the window and Tabitha is playing on my desk, looking outside, I guess it would be difficult trying to keep her inside if she decides she wants to go out. Looking under the covers, I'm naked and have to think for a minute but then remember falling asleep on Jacob last night on the floor downstairs.

Wondering what the exciting events are that are coming today with Pete, I spring out of bed. Jacob is already up but I don't hear him in the bathroom. After brushing my teeth I check out my new hair do, it still looks pretty good and I like it. Throwing on a pair of pants and a matching cotton shirt, I run downstairs and spotting my bins by the door, I pull them into the kitchen where Mattie is working at the counter. Hearing me coming she pours me a cup of coffee.

I open the first bin and start to put stuff on the counter then stop myself. "Is it ok?" I look at her. "Of course it is Madonna" she says, looking in to see what else is in there. Sitting and watching me as I unload my treasures, she's smiling approvingly. "I'm so excited" I say, telling her about Pete coming today with a surprise. Who doesn't love a surprise. She just smiles smugly as I go on and on and suddenly I stop ... looking at her. She tries to look innocent but I ask "did you know about this?" Pulling a face she shrugs her shoulders just as Jacob strolls into the kitchen from his office, looking from Mattie to me then back again, he's wondering what just happened.

Pulling him back into his office, I say "I just realized I'm going on and on about all the things you're giving me, does she have money, can she buy herself things if she wants?" Taken aback for a second, he starts to laugh and says "she won't take any more salary from me so I direct deposit money into her account. Don't worry, she has lots of money, she's fine. By the way, Pete will be here at 1:00." Yeah!

When the doorbell rings at 12:25, I run to answer it believing it to be Pete. It's not Pete standing there at all. Surprised, it's one of Rick's favourite clients. Suddenly feeling flirtatious at his surprised expression, I say "Hi Nick, how are you?" Taken aback for a second, still not remembering where he knows me from, he kind of smiles, stumbling, not knowing what to say when Jacob comes to the front door. "Stop teasing Nick, Rick will be mad at you if you lose him a customer." Now he remembers. "Dawn, right?" Holding out my hand I say "hi Nick, nice to see you again. I'll bet you're surprised to see me here."

I didn't explain why I was here but just left him standing. Coming forward, Jacob shakes hands saying "Dawn is my girlfriend and lives here with me." I can't help but laugh, it's nice seeing all these people. 'You're not in Canada anymore Dorothy.'

Nick and Jacob are in his office going over plans for a new house Nick plans to build nearby, Jacob is helping with the design when Pete arrives precisely at 1:00 with loads and loads of boxes.

Showing him up to my desk in the bedroom, I watch as he unpacks a new computer, photo printer, paper of every size with a year's supply of ink, every program available to edit and print your photos. Last, but not least, I spy a new camera box and three lenses. He also has two smaller boxes that he wouldn't let me see.

Not being very technical, I sit back and watch, not really understanding a lot of what he's doing, too mind boggling for me. All he has left to do now is to transfer over my photo files from my laptop to the new computer. He's already installed the new programs and now he's downloading the new camera program on both computers. Nick has left and Jacob is now watching Pete but not for long when he heads down to the kitchen and is opening the mystery boxes.

When Pete has finished we join Jacob in the kitchen. Picking up the camera and looking at the lenses for a few seconds, I go straight to the manual. Laughing, Pete says "looks a lot more complicated than it really is, you can always start with automatic, right." Right! Before we go sit outside with something cool to drink and maybe a snack, Jacob is glancing hopefully over at Mattie who just nods, Jacob says "Pete, why don't you show Dawn and me how to work these."

Smiling, Pete rips open the mystery box and pulls out two new matching cell phones, one pink, one black. "Oh, simple" Pete says and proceeds to say that these babies have everything - internet access, GPS, mp3 player, text messaging plus plus and, of course, you can talk on them as well" he laughs. I'm still standing there, staring at the goings on, not saying anything. Pete goes on to say that he has set us up on a family plan which means the push of 1 button will call the other, me to Jacob, Jacob to me. And you can add phones. Pete also informs Jacob that he has pre-set the phone numbers that Jacob emailed to him earlier today. What... Great, I mean great, another technical device I need to figure out, how did I get to be such a geek? Laughing nervously now, Jacob seems to understand all this and smiles and nods. "I'll explain it to you later..."

I am truly, very spoiled.

8

Rick's New Offices and a Surprise for Me

Mike, an old University buddy of Ricks, also an architect and a builder has joined in partnership with Rick and Jacob. Mike has worked closely with Rick for the past 10 years and has done the construction work on all of Ricks' projects. This planned joint venture with Mike played an important role in Rick deciding to move his business to Mara. Together, they believe they can really make a name for themselves in this industry and as they wanted a very impressive office space, they purchased an historic Century home, very traditional style to this area and standing on an acre of land smack dab in the middle of the city. They enhanced the two storey house to show off what they had to offer but without taking away from the original design, the place looks awesome. Mattie's landscaper son did the gardens and grounds surrounding the building and you couldn't help but want 'one of those' when you saw this place. That's the idea I guess ... Good job boys.

The building is more than twice the size of Rick's previous office, a necessity to accommodate a second set of employees. The set up is such that each department had its own area but they are close enough to each other that it's an easy, convenient working space.

Rick is waiting for Jacob and me at the front door, a big smile on his face. Greeting him warmly, we congratulate him on his beautiful new offices and he is very proud, rightly so, how exciting. Taking me by the arm and slowly turning me around, Elizabeth, my best friend is standing there smiling at me. Ahhh we both yell and jump into each others arms, I am so happy to see her here. "I have missed you so much" we both say in unison and laugh like two little girls, the guys just stand back and watch, shaking their heads. Rick tells us that Elizabeth has decided to join their new team and has moved down here. Wow, what about the 'old boyfriend' I think to myself. Reading my mind, Elizabeth says "he's history, finally caught the cheater." I just nod, we have all been telling her to dump that loser for years, 3 years to be exact. "Oh honey" she calls coyly over her shoulder and Dean, one of Rick's designers, walks around the corner. "Oh, hi Dean" I smile at him, I always liked

Dean and I know he has been in love with Elizabeth forever. Smiling his hello, he walks over to Elizabeth and puts his arm around her waist, at the same time, she holds out her hand displaying a large, solitaire diamond engagement ring. "What" I yell and now me and her with Dean in the middle, are jumping up and down and around and around and around.

My best friend is back in my life and engaged to a great guy, I am so excited I'm giving myself a headache. Walking over to Jacob I bury my face in his chest. Wrapping my arms tightly around him as the others look on, not knowing what's happening, he explains "it's ok, she's just very happy" as he smiles down at the top of my head.

"Well, that's not all" Rick says as he pulls me out of Jacob's arms and starts walking me down the hallway towards the back corner of the house, everyone following. Stopping at a closed door, I read the sign on it ... 'Touch Hearts Photography Studio' Photography by Dawn Elizabeth. By Appointment Only. Quickly turning to look at Jacob, who must have been in on this, he just smiles that quiet smile that drives me wild, the good kind of wild.

Jacob and Rick have put their heads together and designed my studio exactly the way I would have. They thought of everything and more, it is simply fabulous, of course, there is a reason. Rick wants me to do all their advertising photography. He assures me my name will be displayed as big as the company name on every piece, I know he wants me to take the pictures because he has seen some 'magical' ones of mine that he still can't figure out how I took, helicopter or plane and he knows this new business venture will just take off. I know this too and am more than game. Onward and upward with another adventure ...

9

Michael at the Art Gallery

I'm feeling good this morning. The sun is shining in on the white marble kitchen floor and I am dancing to the 50's music on the radio, tea in one hand, remote in the other. "Mattie" I call over to her, "I didn't know you could change the radio through the glass." Rolling her eyes at me, she continues working at the counter, the kitten is jumping around, trying to catch the sun as it glistens off the glass. When the song starts to get a little too loud, Jacob and Nick come walking out of the office, empty coffee cups in their hands. "Oh, sorry guys, I didn't realize you were working in there" I smile, I'm not really sorry. "Good to see you Nick." Nick, in his ever so soft way asks "so, what are you guys up to today?"

Glancing over at Jacob, I smile as I think 'well, we're finally going to go down to the beach, I have a beautiful new camera that I'm anxious to try out, I'm always in photo mode.

Nick has to leave so Jacob and I grab a quick bite in the kitchen with Mattie, get packed with a change of clothes and are off in the big vehicle. On our drive down the mountain side, I ask Jacob if we can make a stop, "I have something I'd like to bye you" I say to him. He slits his eyes at me, glancing sideways while rounding a sharp curve in the road.

"Please, pretty please" I beg, pouting my lips and holding my hands together as in prayer. I know he cannot resist that. Parking, we get out and Jacob stands looking at the front window, hands on hips, like he has never been here before. Good! Inside the same man who looked after Sam and I a few days earlier greets us. Reminding him that he's holding something for me, a light goes on in his head and he reaches around under the counter, pulling up a black, velvet box.

Smiling, he pulls out a black, velvet lined tray on which is laying a mans' gold cross hanging from a thick gold chain. I move back, not sure what Jacob will think but he doesn't move, just stands there studying the tray, then smiling, he gently picks the chain up in his big hand. "Thank you" he says, turning towards me, "I love it, it's perfect." Quickly walking over to him, I unlock the clasp and putting my arms around his neck, re-fasten the chain. Grabbing my arms before I can back away, he gives my lips a gentle kiss. "Thank you baby." Wow! At least the store owner has the decency to back away and give us a bit of room.

When Jacob and I move away from each other, he quickly comes back with a big smile on his face. Another heart touched. Eyeing my left hand he notices my ring. Ah! he exclaims then shoots a quick look at Jacob. "I recognize this ring" he says with a sparkle in his eye now, "may I clean it for you my dear?" Ok. Moving to the end of the counter, he places my ring in a small, metal box then turns it on, I can hear the tiny motor humming, the box vibrating from side to side. Waiting for this process to finish, Jacob strolls after the elderly man and pretending to look into the jewellery displays, I catch them both in a whispered conversation. Strolling back, he doesn't look at me. The owner walks back a moment later, proudly holding up my shiny ring as if he had just plucked it from the earth. It looks more beautiful than ever. When we get back in the car, I catch Jacob rubbing his new jewellery.

I am so excited. "Can we please make another stop" I cry to Jacob. I got a great idea when I was dancing the other night and I want to act on it. Jacob knows me by now. When I get something in my head, I want to jump on it, if I don't, I won't. This is a good idea, I think a framing place ... or an art gallery.

As it turns out, Jacob knew of just such a place. A very nice Art Gallery, situated in an old, historical, three story house with framing done on the premises. As we walk in, my eyes dart around at all the beautiful art work hanging on the walls. The owner, an older, distinguished, English gentleman, greets us as we enter. Strolling around the main exhibit, I notice some brochures on a desk in the corner. Recognizing them, my heart almost stops.

Picking up the samples with shaking hands, I ask the owner "where did these come from?" He's curious how I know about these but tells me he just bought a painting from New York City and these were wrapped with the painting. I am almost in tears now, remembering.

Inviting us to have a seat, a young girl appears almost immediately with a China pot of hot tea and three delicate cups. Putting the tray on the table, the owner nods his appreciation to her as she steps away. As he pours, he asks me "do you know of this artist?" Focussing my eyes before turning to him, I say "I knew this artist." Jacob shouldn't have been surprised but he was, as well as the owner, who's name we now find out is Andre.

I go on to tell them of my friendship with Michael in Canada. How I knew him for 10 years and how I was the only person they ever invited to their home where Michael painted for 35 years. I had seen finished paintings before they were shipped to the largest art galleries in New York City. How I had been given personal, hand written notes from Michael himself saying what a joy it was for him to see my work ... can you imagine this. How he always said to me "Dawn, some day your prince will come."

"Well" Andre says, "I have something to show you then." Smiling, he leads Jacob and I up an open flight of stairs to a small, personal viewing landing. The sun is being reflecting into the room from a window across the street. As I reach the landing, hanging on the wall is one of the paintings I had seen at Michael's. I was mesmerized by this painting.

Slowly walking towards it, I suddenly feel a pull, something enveloping me and pulling me closer in ... then I hear Michael's voice. He's laughing softly. "I told you Dawn, some day your prince would come." "I love you Michael" I say to the air. "Yes, ok, I will, I promise." When the spirit of the painting releases me, I slowly back away. Standing still for a moment, I then turn to Andre who had stepped back, not quite understanding what just happened. "I'll be in touch" I say to him. "Take care of that painting, do not sell it. You are a very fortunate man." I knew Michael would bring him good fortune.

Turning to leave, Jacob has that knowing smile on his face. He had seen it and couldn't question the things that happen around me. Walking up close to Jacob, studying his face, I lean up and kiss him softly on the lips. "Michael told me he brought me here and always promised me that one day my prince would come." Smiling at each another, turning to leave, I glance back at the painting, it's locked itself onto the wall, it's not going anywhere. I watch as Andre inches up to it, a bit nervous I think. Nothing happens.

Once Jacob and I are in the car, he smiles over at me, asking "what happened back there?" At the beach, sitting on the wet sand, I tell him the whole story of Michael. As I'm talking, I start to wonder. Seems like all of these new, spiritual happenings have started since I've been with Jacob, especially here in Mara. "Tell me about your ancestors" I ask him now, thinking maybe some of this is coming from them.

Jacob stares out at the ocean for a minute, his mind far away. The wind is picking up, the sky is black, the ocean very rough. Cozy now in the warm car, the rain is beating down hard on the metal, lulling us into an hypnotic sleep. Deciding to go home, he talks as he drives.

Jacob grew up happy and spoiled in a large, extended family. He had all that he could hope for and more. He was very smart and finished his architectural degree just before his 21st birthday, just about the time the modeling world spotted him. He was a natural athlete and having spent a lot of time outdoors in the sun, he was not only fit and strong, but blond, tanned and really good looking. The camera loved him so he was always in demand, and you know what they say, men get better looking, more attractive, as they get older.

Laying back, listening to his soft voice, an idea suddenly comes to me. "OK" I say, "I think we have to go see your family." Turning, he stares at me then slowly begins to smile.

On the drive home, the car is tossed around in the strong wind, the heavy rain making it difficult to even see the road. I guess this is going to be one of those days to just cuddle up in bed under the heavy covers. OK by me ...

10

First Photos in New Studio

I am so excited, and surprised, with my new studio, I wonder how long Jacob and Rick have been planning this? As Elizabeth gives me a tour of the rest of the building, I'm looking at the house as it would have been when it was built, I'm guessing maybe 100 years ago. What would the owners' lifestyle have been like back then, no town around it, just land. I can't help but picture houses and buildings as they would have been originally, as they were being built, the ghosts, the families who used to live here. I've always been like this ... I wonder where this came from in me, musing in the past. Hmmm ...

The entire office space is perfectly laid out, very efficient with a great flow. Being a very structured, balanced person, maybe that's why the engineers, designers and I seem to get along so well, so naturally and now all being in the same building, I can just feel my energy soaring, I love it.

There is champagne and cake in the main lobby to celebrate the open house which is starting shortly, I can already see cars pulling into the parking lot, everyone stopping to admire the house and gardens before coming inside.

Picking up a glass of champagne, I wander around the halls and into the offices, to get a personal, up close feel of everything. Noticing a beautifully decorated room across the hall from my studio, the embossing on the crystallized glass door reads 'Interior Design & Staging' by L. Linny. I guess Rick took my suggestion by offering all these great services in one package, but where is this L. Linny and how did Rick find her. I have a feeling this new adventure, of which we all seem to be an integral part of, is going to be a huge success.

Taking my time, I stroll down the hallway before entering my Studio. Rick and Jacob wanted to make the studio a big surprise for me so used the ruse of waiting until the official open house for me to come to the new offices. As my Studio was part of the business and would be open to viewing today, Jacob snuck into my computer and selected some photos that Rick then had blown up and put on display in the main halls. Some were photos of Rick's 'speciality houses,' selected to advertise the business, others were personal and private photographs that Jacob knew would show off my talent as a photographer.

Some of the 'special photos' were the ones that Rick still can't figure out how I took them, amazing pictures, tricky, but possible, in the real world.... Scary to realize how much Jacob and Rick know me. I love them.

When Elizabeth gets a chance, she leaves her 'greeter' position at the front door and runs back to see me where I happen to be standing in the Studio door, deep in thought. When I realized she's there, I give her a warm hug. "It's going to be SO great having you here, what fun we'll have together and Dean, I am so happy" she laughs to me. Smiling back at her, I say "we have a lot to talk about, I'm a great wedding planner and if you agree, I'd like you and Dean to be the first photos I take in my studio, an Engagement picture." "Yes yes yes" she screams jumping up and down.

A few days later I'm back in the studio, my cameras and equipment set up, ready to take my first, official photo and as promised, the engagement picture of Elizabeth and Dean. Elizabeth did a little something special with her hair and makeup and looks even more beautiful, radiant actually. Dean is wearing a dark blue suit with a matching shirt and tie. I've always thought he was very handsome.

As I'm setting them up for the shoot, I ask Elizabeth about this L. Linny, she tells me Lin is the mother-in-law of Kevin who works for Mike. She's an excellent decorator and a really fun person. "I can't wait to meet her".

I snap a lot of photos, some very formal, some really fun, these are the best ones I think. The natural light that comes in from the two corner windows is perfect. After they leave to go back to work, I plug my camera straight into the computer before heading to the kitchen to make myself a welcome cup of tea.

Arriving back at my studio, I see the photos are already displayed on my large flat screen.

Putting my 'jewellers eyepiece' against the screen, I look for clarity in the photos, this 'magic' eyepiece really shows me the sharpest pixels, the best for enlargements. I'm very happy with the results of my first photo shoot, all very nice, of course, having two great looking subjects makes it easy. Oh oh ... here's a picture that I have never seen before, I know I didn't take it and no one else touches my camera, not even Jacob.

Studying it through the eyeglass, now I'm sure I didn't take this photo. It's a picture of five people standing on a country road, spring time, trees just starting to bud, Maple trees I think, horse fencing along the road, grandparents standing, parents kneeling in front, a little blond girl, maybe three, standing in the middle. They all have light jackets on, again early Spring, no snow but dark brown dirt roads? They look like a well-to-do family, healthy, blond. It looks like the little girl is holding a little doll, long blond hair, pink top and shoes, jean skirt, cute ... What! what ... oh oh ... now the little girl is disappearing from the picture.

Quick thinking, I wonder if I can print out a copy of this?

11

The Mystery of the Disappearing Little Girl

Printing out a copy of the photo, I set it in my bag to take home and show Jacob, then carry on with the engagement photos.

I prefer to just take a great picture, not alter it using all the photo enhancement programs that Pete so kindly installed on my new office computer. Yes, I still have another completely loaded, totally compatible computer at home which does come in handy if I start something here at the office then want to finished it at home. With the beauty of the internet, I can also dial from one computer to the other, either way and access, view, even print.

An hour later, I have a variety of colour prints for Dean and Liz as well as a few smaller black and white ones for the newspaper announcements. With the proper lighting, I'm getting hooked on black and whites, I never would have believed it but I do have some beautiful photos of Jacob and Tabitha taken up in our bedroom with only moonlight providing the light. They are awesome and now I'm anxious to take more.

Picking up my empty tea cup and the prints for Liz, I turn to walk out of the studio and standing there, leaning against the door jam, is the love of my life. Dropping everything back on my desk, I walk over to him, arms outstretched. "I was just coming to look for you" I say as he kisses the top of my head, pulling me in close to him. Standing there for a minute or two, breathing together, I feel the need to re-energize from him. "Take a look at the prints I just finished for Dean and Liz" I say to Jacob, "I'm going upstairs, I'll be right back."

Sitting at my desk, looking at the prints, he smiles and says "nice job" as I grab my purse and camera bag, locking the studio door behind us. Dropping the envelope with Liz on our way out we head for the car. "How about lunch at that nice beach restaurant" he asks "we can sit outside on the sand." Sounds good to me.

Seated under a large umbrella right on the sand, a nice bottle of chilled white wine on the table, Jacob said "I've got something for you." "Oh! You've already given me a lot of nice stuff" I say but always happy to be receiving a gift. "Well, this is a little something I picked up in Hawaii but never got around to giving it to you.

Call it a wedding gift maybe" he shrugs. A wedding gift! Feeling guilty as Jacob pushes a small box across the table to me, smiling he says "open it." Inside is a silver and diamond starfish hanging on a shiny silver chain. Beautiful and symbolic to me, the very best kind of gift, Jacob knows me well.

Going around to his side of the table, I give him a hug and whisper "thank you baby, it's perfect." "I know" he laughs and taking it from me, opens the clasp and fastens it around my neck. And it is perfect.

Back in my chair I take a sip of wine then remember. "Oh, I have something to show you" I say as he cautiously looks at me through his lashes. Pulling out the picture that appeared on my camera this morning, he studies it carefully for a full minute or two without speaking. "Ok" he says looking up at me with a question in his voice, still holding the picture between his fingers. Reaching across I take it from him, glance at it and say "well, in my camera, the little girl disappears" and to be sure, I reach for the camera which literally jumps off of the table into my hand, then turns itself on to the picture. Watching closely, sure enough, after a few seconds, the little girl disappears. "Well, I think it's clear that something is going to happen to the little girl but what and when ... and where is she now."

Upon hearing Jacob say this, I take the camera back from him and check the date on the picture. It's dated almost two months ago ... Jacob and I look at each other with a surprised look on our faces.

Over lunch, we try to figure out the details of the picture. I tell him my original thoughts, grandparents, parents, maple trees in spring, possibly the East Coast. I hand him the eyeglass and point out the doll in the girls hand. Is this meaningful? And the date on the photo? Does that mean she disappeared two months ago and if so, why are we getting this now?

On our way back to the car, we stop to see what the boardwalk venders have for sale. A vendor had miniature, silver embossed pictures, professionally framed. I read something about these recently and it is an ancient, oriental art. I love a tiny one that shows a sailboat on the water, sailing along the coast, a small town at the waters' edge, nice piece, both items very inexpensive. Time to go home now, I need a nap.

2 Days Later

Standing in the office lobby, waiting for Jacob who is dropping off some plans, I notice my studio door is open, noises are coming from within. Wondering who can possible be in there as no one goes in without me, I walk down the hallway and see Liz standing over a technician who is installing another phone line. When the reception phone starts to ring, she waves ok to me then runs to answer it. As I'm watching this man at work, a small doll falls out of his tool pouch onto the floor right in front of me.

Squinting down at it, not believing my eyes, it's the same doll that the little girl is clutching in my photo. Curious as to how this man fits in, I walk in to introduce myself, hoping he will tell me his name, he doesn't. He just nods and quickly goes back to what he was doing.

Moving in a little closer, hoping to get the doll, he gives me a quick glance, probably wondering why I'm so close to him now. Success, I was able to slide the doll behind me, away from him and over to where my bag is sitting by the door.

He's almost finished when Jacob appears at the door asking "ready?" "Yes" I say, reaching down to grab the doll along with my bag. "Will you take these for me?" I ask Jacob, standing with my back to the man so he can't see what's in my hand. Rolling my eyes at Jacob, meaning get out of here, he glances down and recognizing the doll, shoves it in his pocket as he takes my bag and heads down to hall. "I'll wait for you outside" he calls back.

Waiting outside both Jacob and I watch as the man leaves with his tool bag. Reaching for my camera bag, once again the camera jumps into my hand. Looking at the picture, this man is definitely not in it. Kicking myself now, why didn't I take a photo of the man when he was here.

As I'm locking up, Jacob learns that the phone tech is from a local phone company and now Rick is curious as to why we are so interested in this man.

I'm thinking and talking a mile a minute on our drive home. "It has to be a kidnapping" I'm saying to Jacob "but where do we go from here? With no evidence other than a 'magic' picture and a common doll, the authorities would laugh us off the block. Let's do some investigating ourselves."

It was easy for Rick to get us information on 'the man' from the telephone company. He kind of thought it was a strange request when Jacob asked but then just went ahead with it, no more questions. Because of all the business Rick gives the phone company, it was only too easy for him to casually ask about our man, saying what a good job he did for us and possibly requesting him in the future.

Careful not to overplay his hand and bring interest back to us, we found out the guy asked for a transfer to the West Coast from New York City about two months ago. He says he is single but some of his co-workers think he may have a daughter. He's staying at the Beaches which is full of families. That's about all we could find out about him.

At home, I decide to take another look at the picture, see if anything else comes to me. East Coast ... kidnapping ... Wouldn't we have seen or heard something in the news, on tv, a missing person list. Surely if a small child was kidnapped, they would do everything they could to get her back. I'm not very good surfing the web but decide to start by looking at the New York City newspapers for the last few months, Jacob is also looking. There is so much news published in this huge newspaper, after an hour or so, we finally figured out how to narrow the search down.

The human interest stories come grouped together if you type in the right words, the right way. Pulling up stories on every way a human can hurt another human from theft to rape to shootings and worse, I try not to read too much detail, almost all of it is bad stuff. One article that did jump out at me for whatever reason, was about a young woman whose body was found in an alleyway. They said she had been beaten to death and that an autopsy revealed she had given birth a few months earlier, she didn't seem to have been a street person. This article was dated almost four years ago.

Finding this very emotional and tiring, I put the kettle on before checking in on how Jacob is doing. He hadn't found anything and is also ready for a break. Sitting outside with the tea and my laptop, I pull up a few comic strips, light, funny stuff. Deciding I needed some entertainment, I pull up the Lifestyle pages and front and centre are the five people from my picture, all smiles, holding a tiny baby girl. Coming around behind me, Jacob reads the article. The date on top of the picture is 3 ½ years ago, the story is of a New York politician showing off his parents, his wife and himself, holding their first grandchild. He was up for re-election that year, the article went on to say, the picture showing a perfect family.

For some reason, my brain kept jumping between the dead woman found in the alley and the picture with the tiny baby. Now my mind is racing ahead, how could I connect the dead woman and the baby, the baby and this family and is she really the same little girl in my picture? If this child was kidnapped by the 'man,' surely that family had the means to search for her, would do everything to get her back. My next step was clear, I would search the newspapers for stories of any kidnapping, ransom demands, etc. Could something like this be kept secret? Would something like this go unreported? And did we know any law enforcement people who could help us?

Over tea, I ran all my wild ideas through Jacob who always did more thinking than talking, the opposite of me. He told me he would make a few phone calls.

Right now? It's about 8:00 pm as he heads into his home office, I'm still sitting on the patio 30 minutes later when he walks back out, shaking his head no. Having no other plan of action at the moment, we are beat so decide to go to bed early, no more computer or phone calls tonight.

Getting into a nice, hot bubble bath together, we try to relax so we can actually sleep, then get into bed and cuddle together. Just about asleep, Tabitha comes running in and jumps on top of us before settling down. Kittens have hot little bodies and even though I'm having a difficult time keeping my eyes open, my brain won't stop. Finally, snuggled up against Jacob, we're both out like a light.

I fall asleep thinking we needed to find a police report on a kidnapping, a search for the little girl. I woke up thinking something entirely different. When Jacob opened his eyes early the next morning, I was already at my desk scanning the birth announcements. We had the mothers name and an approximate birth date. Nothing ... nothing ... and nothing.

Ok, what's next? Well, not everyone puts an announcement in the newspaper, there are lots of reasons why not to. Hospital records. But there are a lot of hospitals in and around New York, where do I start?

Sitting at the kitchen island with Mattie, I remember something. "Mattie, don't you have a niece or someone who's a nurse?" I ask her, maybe now we'll get somewhere.

Yes she did and immediately picked up the phone and dialled her. Listening to Mattie's side of the conversation, I discover there is a central birth registry that hospital personnel can access. Yeah!!! I ran to get the information I had.

We did find out that the child was born in a small hospital in New Jersey on December 24, 2005, the mothers name was on the birth certificate and the father was named as a Mike Peters.

Mike Peters ... that's the name of the telephone technician who was in my office, the same one who dropped the tiny doll. Even though I now had all this information, something told me I had it all wrong but now I was going to take the bull by the horns, probably not the best move but ...

Mike was actually whistling as he walked up the pathway, Jacob met him in the office lobby and led him down to my studio. The cover story was that more electrical work was required and he had been specially requested to do it ... he was starting to feel good about this move to the West Coast.

When he walked into the studio, Jacob closed the door and stood there, arms crossed, an intimidating sight I must say. Sensing something was amiss, Mike quickly looked from Jacob to me then back to Jacob again, now feeling like a caged animal.

I could see him starting to panic so I held out my hand in a calming manner and asked him to have a seat. He sat, both hands gripping the sides of the chair, ready to spring. Taking a step back from him, I slowly hold up my hand .... and in it ... is the tiny doll. No one is saying a word.

"Tell me about this" I say to Mike, when he hesitates I add "we're on your side, we can help." Jacob and I pull up a chair and sit huddled around the man as he tells us of his girlfriend getting pregnant then agreeing to adopt out the baby to some politician in the Big Apple. When they got back together, she changed her mind about the adoption and the next thing he knew, she was dead and the baby was gone. He figured out what had happened and tried to get his daughter back but he was up against a powerful man with lots of contacts and money. The only thing he could do was to grab her and run, and that's just what he did. Now he was hiding out here on the West Coast. 'What kind of future did they have now?' he wondered.

What kind of future did they have now. Mike's words kept running over and over in my head, the future of a child. 'You are here to correct the future of a child' I hear a voice saying in my head and I know. Glancing over at Jacob, he's watching me ... and he nods.

Mike, Jacob and I drive down to the Police Station together. With all our combined pieces of the puzzle, the man who killed the mother and kidnapped the baby girl, would be convicted and sent to prison for a long time, his public career over. Mike's testimony would be the final piece of a puzzle the New York City Police have been working on for years. Mike and Noel Lily would be safe and free to live a happy life. Big Mike, Rick's construction partner, offered Mike P. a job with the company as an electrician, his skilled trade, so we would be seeing him and Lily a lot more in the future. Win win....

We left Mike with the officer and walking along the path to our car, I stopped to give Jacob a little curtsy saying "well done my lord." Laughing he clicks his heels together, bends at the waste replying "my lady." Feeling this particular adventure is over, another happy ending so to speak, I check my camera. There is one picture on it, it's of Mike holding Noel Lily ... The ghost of a pretty blond lady standing behind them, everyone is smiling. And then the entire picture fades to black.

12

The Proposal

Two days later we're on our way to Hawaii. Because
of the popularity of the Islands, there are lots of daily
flights. Jacob knows I don't love flying so booked us
on a well known airline, the plane is new and mid size.
Greeting us at the door, the stewardess leads us forward
to the first class cabin. The pilots' cabin is directly in
front of us and with the door open, we can see the
controls and through the front windshield. Kind of nice
and scary at the same time. As soon as I feel the hum of
the engine, my body starts to vibrate. I'm reminded how
much I hate flying.

Feeling me tense up, Jacob immediately takes my
hand, giving me a smile, he loves to fly. When the
captain boards the plane, he stops to shake hands with
Jacob saying "nice to see you again," nodding to me, a

nice father figure. Ok, I feel a little better now. A minute later we're speeding down the runway, our tires leaving the ground.

Starting to relax, I think I prefer a smaller plane, somehow I feel more in control. Control, what a laugh. The plane is almost full, people seemed to have gotten into the booze already, vacationers. Jacob, being more quiet than usual, turning sideways in his seat, takes my hand. Sounding very serious, he says "I wanted to do this a long time ago but... I was afraid" and lowering his eyes, I look down to see what he's looking at. In his right hand he's holding a blue ring box, still closed. Looking up he continues "I want to give this to you as a sign of my deep love for you. I would love for you to accept it, and wear it, as a sign of your love for me. I want this to be our commitment to each other and when we're both ready, without a doubt, I want to marry you. I want you to want to marry me, I love you so much." I could feel his heart beating as I sat there stunned. Now he's holding up the most beautiful diamond, engagement ring that I had ever laid eyes on.

Looking from Jacob's face watching me, to the ring then back to the face, it dawns on me that I haven't given him an answer. Yes, yes, yes I cry! A quick flash of relief crosses his eyes before giving me a big bear hug. Realizing he is still holding the ring, he gently placed it on my left hand, tenderly touching his lips to mine.

Apparently, the stewardess was in on this, the champagne ready to pop. In her excitement, the cork blows off, hits the ceiling and now the foaming bubbly is spraying all over Jacob's back. Laughing, she poured us a glass, serving it on a tray.

"We have an engagement" she announced to the passenger behind us on the plane. To my surprise, people call out their congratulations, holding up their glasses in a toast then calling for us to make an appearance. Having no escape, we walk to the curtain, hand in hand. Calls to see the "rock" make me lift my hand and show off the sparkler. It was nice of them to make a fuss. As we return to our seats, we hear the captain over the loudspeaker say "congratulations Jacob and Dawn and welcome to Hawaii everyone." The island was just coming into view. 'Wow' I'm thinking to myself, 'what an exciting day.' We were both so happy, neither of us could wipe the smile off our face.

13

The Proposal
Part 2. The Ring
& the Camera

As we exit the plane, the captain is waiting for us on the tarmac. Shaking hands with Jacob, he congratulates him again then gives me a big, fatherly hug. "Thank you Captain Bob" I said without really thinking. "How did you know my name was Bob" he asks with a puzzled look on his face. "No one has called me that since I was in the British Air Force." Stopping in my tracks, a strange feeling comes over me. "Did you by any chance fly with a man names Michael Davies?" "Michael Davies" he laughs. "I sure did. My best pal back in England, always drawing and sketching. He moved to Canada. Gee, I haven't thought of Michael for years." He's smiling as he says this, reminiscing but now he's stopped smiling and looking at me, a small quiver slowly runs through his body. "I knew Michael, he was an artist." By now I'm getting choked up and tears are starting to moisten my eyes. Holding back as best I can, I tell Bob that Michael passed a number of years ago. Reaching out to touch his hand as he lowered his eyes, I knew I would be seeing this man again.

Jacob ordered a classic vintage, red and white convertible for our stay. Pulling out of the parking lot, we jump on the expressway heading into downtown Honolulu where Jacob's booked us a beautiful suite at one of the finest hotels. The 37th floor suite with a full view of the ocean, is larger than any apartment I've lived in and is beautiful. Washing up, changing our clothes, we head down to the formal dining room on the 5th floor, also with a balcony overlooking the ocean.

Tired from all the excitement but starving, I can't remember when I had last eaten. The dining room has a very high, vaulted ceiling, full of bright crystal chandeliers, tiny white lights everywhere, the tables are set with beautiful china and silverware, a very formal room. I was glad I had decided to wear the simple black dress I had bought with Sam. Even without accessories, I looked terrific. Of course, the shiny new diamond ring on my finger didn't hurt.

Over dinner and, of course, wine, Jacob and I talked about the days happenings. It was finally sinking in for me, I was truly happy and loved Jacob very much. He told me he had been thinking about getting me something special a few months ago and found himself in front of Andres', the jewellery store we both seem to be drawn to.

When he walked in and told Andre he really had no idea what he was looking for, after contemplating a moment, Andre lead Jacob over to the Estate jewellery. Looking into the glass display case, he pulled out a small, dark blue velvet tray, on it were two vintage pieces that had Andre puzzled, he received them just a few short weeks ago.

The jeweller told Jacob that he purchased a lot of his vintage pieces through the internet because they came from all around the world. He doesn't remember seeing or ordering these two and couldn't even find invoices for them. He found a description on one sheet of paper but no price or where they came from. Not knowing what to do, he put them into his display case. They always seemed to end up beside each other. In the same shipment he found a jewellers eyepiece, it seemed to be an older style and didn't work very well on the jewellery but did wonderfully when placed against the computer screen, to view items for sale on line. Curious ...

Jacob was drawn. Picking up the engagement ring, examining it closely, he wondered if Dawn would like it.' It was a truly beautiful ring, 6 diamonds and two blue German sapphires the jeweller told Jacob, assuring him that he had tried to authenticate the origin of the ring but could only be sure of the quality of the stones and gold, the highest quality. There was a mark on the inside of the band but for some reason, Andre couldn't quite make it out.

Putting the ring down on the velvet cloth, Jacob picked up the Sapphire and diamond band. Another beautiful ring and he knew Dawn was partial to sapphires. How to decide. Studying both of them laying on the velvet, were his eyes deceiving him. They seemed to have moved towards each other. Blinking, they were definitely closer to each other. A ring in each hand now, he definitely felt a small charge go through his fingers, then between each other. Smiling, he tells the jeweller "well, I guess I'm going to take both." Andre is delighted. A strange feeling settled over Andre as he was placing the ring boxes into a small gift bag before adding in the antique eyepiece. Something just told him to do so. Jacob was whistling as he left the store.

As Jacob is telling me this story, I take off the diamond ring and start to look inside the band. There is something written in there but I can't quite make it out. Do you have the jewellers eyepiece, I ask him. Rolling his eyes, he smiles, knowing I would ask for it. Reaching into his jacket pocket, he hands me a black object, about 1 ½" in length, curved, a bit larger at one end. I think it's made of some type of ceramic, heavy for its size and very old, well used. I hold it sideways to the light to see if any fingerprints are on it. None!! What am I, a detective now. Too much tv. :)

Putting the eyepiece up to my eye then to the band, at first everything is blurry. Coming into focus, in an italicized font and almost worn off, I read 'To S from M.D.' My mouth drops open as I pass the ring to Jacob.

Now he can read the inscription easily without the eyepiece. "This was not here before, I looked at the jewellery store." Quickly taking off the first ring Jacob gave me, I look inside *'To S. Love M.D.'* "Oh my God" I breath, holding my hand up to my mouth. Jacob takes that ring from me and looks inside. "Wow" he whispers. OK, what is happening. Putting my rings back on before I misplace or lose them, I have an urge to reach into my purse and pull out my new camera. I really didn't want to drag the whole camera bag into the formal dining room, but could not seem to leave the room without it or could not leave it in the room, alone....

Unable to resist, I pull it out of my purse but attached to the camera where a strap would go, is a narrow, brown leather and well worn strap that I have never seem before. It looks to be the type we used years ago, the type you had to undo, wrap around, feed through then almost button on. Once you put it on and adjusted it to your neck, you never took it off. So was I losing my mind? And is that white paint on the strap. By now, Jacob is just watching me ... and drinking lots of wine.

I'm almost afraid to touch the camera now. For some reason, since I've had it, I have not taken even one picture with it. That kind of scares me. Am I losing my passion. Well, now I am curious so studying the camera, familiarizing myself with it, I'm about to turn it on when suddenly it turns on by itself and a picture instantly appears on the screen.

Not entirely sure what the picture is, it looks like a pit dug into the earth with branches almost covering it. I see trees right behind it and... do I hear calling for help? What is this, a video? Pressing the display button to see if there are any more pictures either before or after this one but nothing, this is the only picture in the camera. Pulling out the memory stik that I watched Pete unwrap from the sealed package and put in the camera, I press the display button to check if the picture is in the camera's memory but nothing. Putting the memory stik back in, I pull up the picture. Pressing another button will display the date and time the picture was taken. What the ...... the date is two days from now. Ok, no better time that the present to check out your new camera. Going into Set up mode, sure enough, the date and time are right, actually to the minute of right now, ok, back to the picture display and yup, the date is two days from now. I am talking aloud this whole time so Jacob sees me checking and double checking my facts and he also just doesn't know. So now what? Showing him the picture again to see if he can make it out, all he can guess is that it's a picture of an animal trap. Could the picture have come with the camera, like when you buy a fame. I don't think so. When we get upstairs, I want to phone Pete.

Well that was an interesting dinner. Missed the atmosphere, the sun setting over the balcony that was 20 feet from us. Great food and wine though and I think Jacob is on board with whatever adventure seems to be happening to us, both of us for we both feel that Jacob is included now since the incident at the jewellery store involved him directly. And besides, Michael could use him to get to me. I get the feeling that Jacob is Michael's prince, meant for me all along.

I have a feeling something magical is going to happen here in Hawaii.

"Hi Peter, aloha from Hawaii" I call into my cell. "Sorry to be calling so late but I have a question for you, about my new camera.... Where did you get it from?" This direct question kind of takes Peter off guard for a second. "Well, I remember exactly where I got it. When Jacob told me what he wanted to buy you, what you would be using it for, your passion for photography, I looked around my stock room to see what I might have in the way of camera equipment that you might like.

I found this box almost hidden behind a new shipment I'd just put away. I'm pretty sure it wasn't there before and I don't know what made me look there now but when I saw the old box, I had to take a closer look. Pulling the camera out of the box, it was not like the one pictured on the cover, it was a new, modern and fully loaded, camera with some stuff I have never seen before, really neat features.

All the modern memory sticks and lenses fit perfectly so I put a kit together for you, new batteries as well. I think the box is still at the store." "OK, Pete, did you check to see if there were any pictures in the cameras' memory or did you take any pictures? I saw you open the stick and install it at our place, so there wouldn't have been any pictures already on that but..." "Wait just a minute, this sounds crazy. What are you getting at?" he's laughing to me now.

"Two things..." I answer him back, "firstly, when I opened the bag to take the camera out, there was an old, worn brown leather strap attached to the bag. I don't remember seeing this before at all. Secondly, when I turned the camera on, there was a picture of what looks like a roasting pit, partially covered by branches. The picture was numbered 1 of 1 and dated tomorrow. I checked the set up, the full display and the date and time are correct and there is only the one picture on the camera. I can't figure out where this picture came from. Any ideas?" Not laughing anymore, Pete says "Wow, this certainly sounds like a mystery to me."

Remembering something else I say to Pete excitedly "Oh, that isn't all, Jacob and I are engaged." By now I am wired from the late night, wine at supper and all the happenings, the good ones and the strange ones. I hear him yelling to his wife, both of them are congratulating us. Jacob is watching me from the bed, a smile on his face. I don't tell Pete about the inscription on the rings, he doesn't know the whole picture story so it would be too confusing for him. Well, he wasn't any help with the picture in the camera or the strap, the mystery continues.

Both of us are very tired now so it's nice to crawl into the big, soft bed, our warm bodies curling around each other. Our first night as an engaged couple.

14

Solving the First Picture

The sun is shining brightly into the room when I hear Jacob talking to someone. Rubbing my eyes open I see him standing in the half open doorway wearing only his boxer shorts, hair sticking up. I can see a breakfast trolley in the hallway and hearing another voice, for some reason I look around for my camera, spotting it on the table in the other room. Throwing off the covers to go get it, suddenly it's beside me on the bed. As I pick it up, it turns itself on and focuses. Hearing the music coming from the camera, Jacob cocks his ear in my direction.

"Good morning" I call as Jacob pushes the door wider showing a young man standing there. Aiming my camera at the door, I push the button. The young man is surprised to see a lady sitting up in bed in her pj's, taking his picture, Jacob doesn't seem surprised at all. I notice that the new black strap is now attached to the camera, I'll have to ask Jacob if he put it on. Telling the young man to wait a minute while he goes for his wallet, I ask him where he's from, where his family is. He names a village on the island and I notice he's trying to cover up his left hand, which seems to be burned. When I ask him how long he's worked at the hotel, because he looks very young, he tells me "only three weeks. There was an accident at his home and he's working, trying to help out his family." He seems too young to be away from his home and family. Jacob nods when he tells him his family name, seeming to know them.

"Goodbye Raoul" I say as he backs out of the door, holding his tip money. My thoughts are spinning ahead of me and looking at Jacob, I can see his mind spinning as well. Sitting at the hot breakfast laid out in front of us, I display the picture I just took. Coming around behind me to look, this is not the one I just took. Raoul is not wearing the hotel jacket but a white shirt and blue tie, a school uniform. He's waving to us with a good left hand, no burn. The picture changes before our eyes and now, behind him, are plantation trees. Jacob is watching over my shoulder, just smiling. "You're planning on talking to your uncle about his father, aren't you" I ask Jacob. Picking up a fresh piece of pineapple he just smiles.

The fruit smells terrific and wondering if it's from his family's plantation, looking over at me he nods, his mouth so full he's unable to talk. "Do they know who you are?" I ask. "Yup." I love a man of few words, the strong, silent type. It seems during the last week or so Jacob and I are on the same wave length, I wonder if he can actually read my mind.

He's watching me... Does this strong spiritual connection between us come from his ancestry ... and who knows who or what has now awakened it. I tell him about looking for the camera earlier and it coming to me in bed and turning itself on. Raising his brows, he doesn't say anything.

Breakfast finished, we jump in the shower together, a first for us. The bathroom is so big and at first I'm a little shy but Jacob is so casual and actually funny. After doing my hair and putting on a touch of makeup, remembering I'm meeting his grandparents today, my heart gave a little jump as my fingers touch the rings on my finger.

Wow, I love Hawaii, I may never want to leave. Jason tells me that after we spend some time with his family, maybe we'll drive around the island and spend a few days somewhere, a little vacation. "How does that sound?" he asks. 'How does that sound ... YES !!!'

His family's plantation is an hour's drive away. I don't know what I was expecting when Jacob said his family owned a plantation that has been supplying fruit to the U.S. and Canada for over 100 years, their name is known worldwide. I had no idea what to expect but started to laugh when we pulled up to a iron gate and had to buzz then wait to be let in.

The huge main house sits at the far side of a wide, circular driveway. Standing two floors high with a wide

D.E. Payne

balcony all around, each room opens to the outside as well as onto a centre courtyard. A three car garage is off to one side. Tall, lush vegetation full of colourful and fragrant flowers and birds fill the yard. On the veranda, wicker furniture is stuffed with colourful cushions as well as a long, old wooden table surrounded by straight backed chairs. It seems almost everything is done out of doors. Shear, natural fibre curtains hang along the veranda and blow in the warm breeze. Walls, inside and out, are white and the roofs seems to be covered with banana leaves, very tropical. There is even a hammock in the far corner. Wonderful ...

As we pull the car up to the house, women swarm out through the wide, double doors onto the veranda, kids run straight up to the car, assuming Jacob would stop in time and not hit them. He does stop then lots of yelling and greetings are exchanged before we're even out of the car. The first thing Jacob does is come around to my side, open my door and help me out of the car. Thankfully, he doesn't take his hand off my arm but introduces me formally to each one in turn. They hug and kiss both Jacob and me, they seem like a truly loving family. The entire time, the kids are running in between and through us, Jacob spoke to them to quiet down and they listened and were very polite.

Before heading into the house, Jacob opens the trunk and pulls out a large box, gifts for all the kids. When did he do shopping? Inside, where it's a little cooler, we all sit down to a large picture of sweet iced tea. The men will be back from the fields soon and we can enjoy some time together over supper.

The grandmother and cousins kept talking over each other, catching up with what Jacob is doing. He seems to be enjoying it as much as the ladies and I enjoy watching him in this different setting. Catching his old grandmother looking at me, when I ask Jacob about it, he smiles sheepishly and nods. Suddenly, her eyes open dramatically and grabbing my left hand, she inspects the ring. A huge smile breaks out on her face then taking my face in both her hands, she kisses me on each cheek. Jacob laughs, the cousins laugh then she touches the ring and a shock shoots through the ring to her and back to me. Shocked, we stare at each other then I find myself showing her my other ring, the diamond and sapphire one on my right hand. Again, she gingerly touches it and the same thing happens.

Before I can even blink, she's excitedly talking to Jacob and the girl cousins and I have no idea what's happening. She stops talking as suddenly as she has started, bents down to look into Jacob's eyes, then comes over to me, grips me by my arms and looks me straight in the eyes. Starting to be afraid, I glance at Jacob and he seems to be saying "here we go again." Oh no!!!

At that moment, we hear vehicles pulling up to the house, a few seconds later, three men walk into the kitchen, I'm assuming the grandfather and cousins. They all greet Jacob warmly, play punching his arm and tousling his hair like he's the young cousin, which he is. He doesn't seem to mind. Getting the urge to take a picture of the guys just the way they are, coming in from work and Jacob casual, my camera is on the coffee table.

Picking it up, it feels a bit hot, maybe it's been sitting in the sun, but no, there's no sun on this side of the room.

Waiting for the guys to finish their greetings and Jacob to introduce me, the camera is getting awfully warm. Checking it all over, wondering what in a camera could be producing heat, batteries maybe, lost in thought, I glance up and my eyes are automatically drawn straight out through the kitchen door to the back yard. I recognized the view immediately, it's the picture from the camera. From where I'm standing, the pit is at least 100 yards away and catching a movement, I walk to the kitchen door to get a better look. A tiny spot at the edge of the pit seems to be moving.

Suddenly I find myself running out the back door, screaming for Jacob. Sensing the urgency in my voice and the fact that I'm racing out the back door, he runs after me. The men and the women automatically start to run after us, not knowing why. When we reach the pit, looking in, we see a small boy hanging onto the long grass, clinging close to the top of the pit. His feet are hanging only inches from the fiery bottom, I can feel the heat from where I'm standing. What I saw moving was a tiny white kitten.

Getting down on his knees, Jacob reaches over and grabbing the small body with his large hands, pulls him up and out of the hot trench. By the time he carries him around the pit and places him on the ground, the boy is surrounded by all the relatives, checking every body part on him.

The conversations are fast and furious, the boy just lays there, stunned. Seeing that the boy and Jacob are ok, I turn and walk towards the orchards at the back of the yard.

With my back against a tree, I sink to the ground. What just happened? The camera, the picture, a prophecy. I had begun to believe that the picture was somehow put there by Michael but now ... Was it a sign for me to watch for, maybe if I was in the right place at the right time, I could be of help? Maybe Michael was directing me to where bad things were going to happen and I could stop it, save someone, help. And Jacob seems to be involved somehow.

Sitting there on the ground, I feel hot, tired and dirty, totally whipped, drained. How long have I been sitting here, lost in my own thoughts. Looking up, I see Jacob sitting on the grass, his arms around the small boy, the women are also sitting on the ground, crossed legged, listening tentatively to Jacob, who seems to be telling them a story. He keeps glancing over at me and seeing that I'm alright, keeps talking to the women. The men are standing behind them, also listening, one of them has gone into the house for something. The boy didn't seem to be hurt with the exception of a couple of red area on his elbows and knuckles from the heat when he fell in. His clothes are dirty as are Jacob's. I think he's kind of enjoying being the centre of attention, now that everybody is no longer yelling at him, telling him all the awful things that could have happened to him. Being upset is now replaced by thankfulness that he is alright.

Holding my head in my hands, my eyes burning, I sense someone standing in front of me. Slowly looking up, I find the boy and his father, the father has his hands on his sons' shoulders, the boy shyly looks up at me and says "thank you for saving me. I was very afraid but that little white kitten sat on the grass and kept saying "hold on, hold on." Staring at him, my eyes wide, my mouth open, this is becoming too much for me now. Smiling weakly at him, his father smiles back at me and they both walk away towards the house. The women are now heading in that direction as Jacob ambles over to me, plopping down on the grass, he puts his arm around my shoulders. Looking each other in the eyes, we both take a deep breath then smile. Studying his face then following down the line of his shoulders and arms, he's very dirty and has a few hot spots of red on him. "Are you ok?" I ask, very concerned. I remember him dropping to his knees at the edge of that hot pit, then reaching in to grab the little body hanging there.

My hero. My heart is aching with love for him and concern. He nods humbly in answer to my question. "Are you ok" he asks, concern showing on his face. "I am now" I say, leaning forward to touch his lips, he leans towards me. "I had to tell them about the picture in the camera. They knew something was happening and that explained it all to them. They say you have an spirit with you, guiding, directing you. My grandmother felt it in the rings as well. She believes we have a strong, spiritual connection." He smiles. "She thinks we need to be married as soon as possible." He says this and quickly looks away, afraid of my reaction.

Looking at his profile, trying to judge his reaction, I look off into space for just a second ... to contemplate. Contemplate the signs, signs all around us, me and Jacob, even our friends are involved. I feel these are good signs. Good signs indeed.

"Yes" I say aloud, still facing forward. Spinning around he looks at me, his mouth open, unbelieving, then he slowly starts to smile. "Well, OK then." Standing up, he pulls down his shirt, very seriously looking then grabbing my hands, he scoops me up into his arms, kissing my face all over, laughing. "She said yes" he yells to the sky. In my excitement I throw my arms up and the camera goes flying high. Oww I yell but Jacob, looking up, cups his hands and catches it, safe and sound. I can't believe I just did that. Breathing a sigh of relief, we suddenly stop and look at each other ... "did you hear a click" we say at the same time.... but now we're afraid to look.

Turning towards the house, I catch his grandmother's face in the kitchen door, watching us and smiling.

15

The Wedding Day

Waking up the next morning, I'm alone in bed. Jacob's not an early riser so I'm wondering where he's gotten off to when one of the patio doors open and he slips in. Quietly pushing the door closed, he smiles as he opens his arms. "Tabitha" I yell as she jumps out of his arms and into mine, happy kisses and licks all over my face.

"How and when did she get here?" I ask. "Mattie flew in this morning, I called her yesterday, she wouldn't have missed this for the world." He smiles, thinking of his long time adopted mother and friend. "We just got back from the airport." I must have been dead to the world to not know he wasn't at my side in bed. I seem to be getting extra senses since arriving in Hawaii and just don't seem to want him out of my sight, something he usually accommodates me with.

Sitting on the side of the bed, he gives me a little kiss, Tabitha is jumping all over us, happy, she missed us I think. Jacob tells me that today I am to just sit back and let myself be pampered. Tradition says that the day of a brides wedding, everything is done for her and to her, to get her ready for the ceremony tonight. Starting from the moment I walk out of this room, ladies and girls will be not only waiting on me for my daily activities, like breakfast but they'll be preparing a special bath with spiritual essence and lotions, doing my nails, hair and makeup. Fitting me with the ceremonial dress and Lai, also the dress I'll wear after the ceremony. The whole day is surrounded with tradition, which they will explain to me in detail as we go. Being a detailed person, I'm thrilled to be able to fully appreciate this entire day.

Everyone has this "very special" day off and want to be involved in the blessing so are busy preparing a feast for tonight as well as picking special white orchids which are grown on the plantation. Picking up Tabitha when I hear people at the door, Jacob asks me if I'm ready. Not only am I ready, I'm anxious. "No doubts?" I ask him. "No doubts" he answers, smiling. 'Let the day begin' I think to myself as I open the door. Mattie is standing there, arms wide open.

This day has been so awesome I can't believe it. I've been led from place to place and every wish or desire has already been thought of and more. As I'm seated at my wedding breakfast (alone for Jacob cannot see me at any time today), activity is happening all around me. People fill the kitchen either bringing in or preparing food.

Lights and flowers are going up everywhere inside the house and out, I can see the backyard is being transformed. Tents, tables and chairs, flowers everywhere and large speakers are being set up in the gazebo. Where did all these people come from and how was all this organized so quickly? The entire day is filled with wonderful traditions, I am so happy and feel that there's a good spirit around me, I can't describe it ... I ate all day.

The ceremony starts at sunset with everyone walking from the plantation house to the top of the cliff where the old ancestral church stands. As it grows darker, you can see a path of candles moving up the hillside. A white, wooden archway stands on top of the cliff, long strips of white silk flow from it and beautiful flowers surround the posts, the place smells terrific. At the bottom of the cliff, waves crash high on the rocks. A truly spectacular view with the sun setting over the ocean. 'Click'

As Jacob and I stand facing each other and holding hands under the archway, a local holy man starts the ceremony. I admit to not really listening to him as my mind is racing. My eyes are drawn towards the little chapel where Michael is standing. Dressed in his usual dark slacks and short sleeved white shirt, he doesn't have his tie on but a flower lei. Smiling at me, he touches the fragrant flowers, his way of congratulating us. Now beside him appears great-grandfather, also smiling and nodding. Putting his arm around Michael, they seem to be together. Curious.

When I look back at Jacob, his eyes are smiling at me knowingly. Even though he can't see what I see, he is seeing it through my mind, my eyes, and I had missed my entire wedding ceremony ... or had I? 'This was better' I think to myself and feeling Jacob chuckle, for him too I guess.

Now that the Minister has stopped talking, everything seems quiet. Turning, I see Mattie holding up my camera then hear a 'click," she just smiles. Looking up, the sky is full of stars, seeming to concentrate right above us, like they're smiling. Jacob and everyone else is looking up as well and 'click.'

Then Jacob, laughing out loud, grabs me and gives me a big kiss. Crying out, the guests throw up their arms and we feel our bodies being hit with something soft and sweet smelling. Orchids, lots of beautiful, fragrant orchids ... then the kids run to gather them up from the ground and walking carefully to the edge of the cliff, throw them over into the ocean. Jacob explains that this is like throwing rice back home. They are love and good wishes from our family and friends, covering us and then flowing out into the universe. Wow.

As we turn to head down the hill, Jacob glances towards the crowd, seemingly looking for someone then he breaks into a wide smile. Walking towards us is a tall black man all dressed in white, followed by a large, white stallion. Throwing themselves into each others arms, I've never seen Jacob look so happy. His friend doesn't look too bad either.

Jacob introduces me to his very best, long time friend and his friend introduces me to the horse... then both men help me up onto its back and away we go, heading down to the plantation house and the party. As I move away on the stallion, I hear Jacob say "after you princess." 'Princess?' and I hear Michael's laughing voice in my head "some day your prince will come." Jacob is smiling that quiet, knowing smile. "Well, when you marry a prince...."

We can hear the plantation before we see it, the place is rocking, the party has begun.

Everyone is having a good time, eating, drinking, dancing to the music. As is tradition, I go inside to change into a different dress, a long flowing white on white two piece tunic style with sleeves that hang down over my hands, hem dragging on the ground. A very thin, almost invisible band of greenery around my head. When I come back outside, Jacob and Morgan are sitting at a small, round table, each with a glass of champagne in their hand and one on the table for me.

Another long table is full of every kind of food you could imagine, wine and beer and a beautiful white three tier wedding cake decorated with sea shells is front and centre. Flowers and candles are everywhere, music fills the air and people are dancing. As I sit down, Jacob is saying "I never thought this would happen to me" as Morgan laughs and says "hey, I didn't think you were ever coming back." "What are you guys talking about?" I laugh, taking a sip of champagne.

"Well" Morgan starts, "Jacob has been filling me in on some of the things that have been happening to you two so I'm sure what I'm going to say will come as no surprise. Jacob, don't you find it odd that I have appeared every time you were in any kind of trouble, ever since you were a very young boy?" Jacob makes a face as he acknowledges this is true. He's starting to remember more and more. "Well, I've been a protector over your family and you for a very long time. I'm really Sir Morgan, one of the knights assigned to protect the prince, that would be you Jacob. You and Dawn were meant to be together and it just took a little bit of manipulation to make it happen. When you arrived together on the island, all powers gathered and things started to happen, especially between you two. I assume you can read each others minds?"

I'm listening intensely and my head jerks up when I hear this. What the .... Jacob glances over at me. "Winston, the horse, is also with me" Morgan laughs. "I always thought he didn't belong in this time" he says as we all look over to where the stallion is eating grass, Tabitha is sitting on his back. I want to rub my eyes, not believing what I'm seeing. Morgan sees me looking and says "Oh, Tabitha is one of us as well." "How can that be, I rescued her as a tiny baby?" "Oh, you rescuing her was in the plan but animals come back as babies and grow up again.

Winston and her know each other but not as well yet as they did last time when they lived together for years." Have I had too much champagne already. I need to sit back and think about this for a minute. "We'll have lots of time later and tomorrow to get into this, now it's party time" Morgan says, standing up and walking over to the mike.

16

The Wedding Night

I woke up with an arm around my waist, a warm body against my back and a rough chin against my ear, then I realized I also had a tiny, fury face rubbing my other cheek. Snapping my eyes open, Tabitha is laying there all curled up fast asleep and purring, much like she does at home. Whoa... I knew we didn't bring her with us last night, did Mattie bring her here this morning? Feeling me move, Jacob opens his eyes and spies her on the pillow. Sitting up on one elbow, he says tenderly "Tabitha, you know we love you but you have to be careful doing this." Doing what? I'm thinking. Climbing up on him, she begins licking his rough face then quickly pulls back, acting like she's got something on her tongue, she doesn't like it ... I guess his whiskers licked back.

"I think she just missed us, she won't be able to do that back home" Jacob is telling me, I'm still trying to figure out what he's talking about. Just then Morgan appears in the balcony doorway, hot coffee in his hand and now he's dressed in black leather. Wow! I can imagine how he must look up on that horse, he must have been a lady killer back in 'his day.'

Explaining to me how animals can move from place to place, he says "they want to be somewhere or with someone and they are there, like Tabitha right now, she probably just wanted to be in bed with you, like she has always done, she went into your bedroom back at the plantation, started to jump up on the bed, expecting you to be there, picturing you there and she landed here, beside you, just as she pictured. She doesn't know any difference but she's growing up now so you need to explain it to her, so she is safe. As Jacob said, she might not be able to do that back in Mara, there's not the magic power there as there is here but she will be able to do some things ...

Morgan has a full breakfast set out in his room so heading in there, Tabitha happily follows. I want to keep her with me for now, we'll send her back when we're ready to leave the hotel. While I'm having my tea, Jacob phones Mattie and update her on Tabitha, she doesn't seem surprised!

Right now, our plan is to hang around our suites, eat, rest up from the last few days, I'm exhausted, and we have LOTS to talk about. As we fill our plates from the antique silver serving trays and goblets, I notice that what we remove is instantly replenished, more and different foods just keep appearing. Wow, I could get used to this.

Birds are flying outside our balcony and calling out over the ocean spray. Sitting on the balcony, Morgan tells us stories of magic. After a few hours of this entertainment, he stands up and walking into his suite, returns wearing a black leather jacket announcing "it's time for me to go." "Oh no" I cry "don't leave." As Tabitha jumps up into his arms, he says "I'll drop her off with Mattie at the plantation and she'll take her home, she's leaving this afternoon. OK? Tabitha."

Looking up at him with love in her eyes, he says to her "I promised didn't I?" Running over to him, I give him a kiss, almost crying to see him leave us. "My lady" he said kissing my hand then shaking hands with Jacob, he bows his head and said "my lord", very formal, very proper then with his right hand, he touches a small silver horse pin on his sword belt and Winston appears beside him. Purring loudly, Tabitha jumps onto the horses back, rubbing her head against his huge head, he rubs her back. Taking the reigns Morgan says "hold on" to the both of them, once again touches the small silver broach and they all disappear. "Oh" was all I could say, they were gone so suddenly.

17

The Morning After ... The Wedding Night

Standing there for a minute, we then turn and walk hand in hand back to bed. Propping myself up with pillows beside Jacob, I suddenly remember "we're married, we're really married." Laughing nervously, the realization is also sinking in to him. "You know" I say coyly, "you haven't ravished your new bride yet, we missed the wedding night." "Then I'll just have to rectify that right now" he laughs. And he does ...

Laying in his arms afterwards, admiring my engagement ring I realize that I didn't have a wedding band, nor did he. When I mention this to him, he says "oh, I forgot, Morgan gave me this" and opening a black leather jewellery box, I see two matching wedding bands. Hmmmm. Lifting out the smaller one, it is inlayed with small sapphires and diamonds, alternating and going around the entire band. I can just make out a faint inscription on the inside, it says to 'Elizabeth from Jacob,' Jacob is watching me, waiting. Smiling at him I ask "how did you know my middle name is Elizabeth?" Shaking his head no, he takes off my engagement ring and places the wedding band on my left ring finger, it fits perfectly, no surprise there. Putting my engagement ring back on in front of the band, it's a perfect match.

The larger ring is identical but the diamonds and sapphires are larger and more widely spaced, it looks very manly. Watching as Jacob inspects the ring, it's kind of different and I'm not sure he likes it. Inside the band is written "no doubts" and Jacob laughs as I slip the ring on his finger. It fits perfectly and feels like it's always been there. We think maybe it has ...

18

Returning Home

When we finally got up, the sun is shining brightly in our room, but something is different. Walking out onto the balcony, we were still in Hawaii, at the hotel but I was standing on a modern, third floor balcony, a large green lawn in front of me filled with trees and flowering plants. The cliffs were a long ways off, there was no mist or spray on my face like last night when we were on the edge of the ocean. It was time to go home.

The magic that had surrounded us yesterday had left with Morgan and we both felt it was time to leave. Deciding to take a leisurely, scenic drive up around the north end of the island and stop at a nice plantation restaurant for the buffet brunch they were famous for. Jacob had already phoned the airport and we had 2 reservations on the 6:00 pm flight which would take us directly to the Mara airport where Mattie would pick us up, a short 20 minutes from home. We had the entire day to enjoy before our flight but already our hearts had left the island.

Driving home from the airport, Mattie told us she had a wonderful time in Hawaii, a nice visit with the family whom she had known for years, even before Jacob was born and it was a truly magnificent wedding, magical she says with a wink. I got the feeling she knew more than we knew she knew.

Putting his arm out to stop me from entering our front door, Jacob carries me over the threshold, laughing. "Oh, how gallant." Mattie is standing back waiting for this nonsense to pass but smiling to herself. After Jacob stops just inside the door, still holding me, I looked down to see Tabitha sitting there, waiting for us, she must have heard us coming. Studying the situation, she easily springs up onto my stomach then proceeds to lean up onto Jacob and give him a rough kiss on the cheek. "Ow" he yelped. Insulted she quickly turns her attention to me and I'm prepared for her rough tongue. She loves us and had missed us. What an adventure for her I thought, or maybe not.

Putting me down, I don't move but look around, something is different, someone had been in our house. Closing my eyes, I get a strong feeling of lots of people and quickly turning to Mattie, panic starting in me, she slowly lowers her eyes and holds up her hand, in that ok, calm down gesture. "It's ok" she says and glances at Jacob.

Slowly walking me up the stairs to the bedroom, Jacob is a few steps behind. Wow! 'Now I understand' I say to myself. On the wall where the wall to wall desk had been, now stands a double glass patio door leading out to a full size, open veranda that runs the length of the bedroom. Opening the doors I step out onto the balcony, Tabitha right behind me. She immediately jumps up onto the railing and runs along its length to sit under the bird feeder that's hanging there, I think she's been out here before. When could all this have been done, we've only been gone 5 days, Mattie and Tabitha for the last 2.

It's beautiful, just what I wanted. The view of the pool and backyard is very different from up here and I can see over the trees almost to the city, breathtaking.

Going back inside I see the desk has been shortened a bit and is now a corner unit, the screen and keyboard sitting on the largest area of desk top. The tower and printer are below on shelves, supplies handily right beside them. The other side is open below so I can sit right in and do my photo stuff. A perfect design I'm thinking to myself but then, what else could I expect from a designer, Jacob.

The other side of the doorway is now freed up and a small, black leather loveseat with a matching cube table is there, the floor lamp has been moved over between the loveseat and the bed, enabling the light from it to cover both areas. Jacob has thought of everything. "Surprise" he says holding out his arms and laughing. Just perfect.

Walking into his arms, I lean up to give him a nice kiss. "Thank you Jacob, it's all wonderful ... and perfect.

I love you." Smiling, feeling good about doing this for me, he whispers "I love you too baby."

Standing at the bedroom doorway, Mattie says "supper's ready" and heads downstairs, we could eat. Following her into the kitchen, we stop in our tracks. The entire room, as well as outside on the patio, is full of beautiful, fragrant flowers. I'm overwhelmed by the love and by the smell that fills the room as Jacob and I open a few of the cards that are attached to the arrangements, not the little cards that the florists write but full Wedding cards. Lots of the cards said 'can't wait for the party' and Jacob and I just smile at each other. Mattie said they starting arriving as soon as she got home and just kept coming, there are also a stack of messages on the answering machine. She just stopped answering the phone she told us.

A nice light supper is set up on the patio table, complete with white wine and Mattie's famous desserts. As I start to close the patio door behind us, Tabitha comes flying through it. "Stop" I say to her, holding up my hand as she slides to a stop and waits for me. Knowing what I now know, I couldn't stop her from getting outside if I tried, even so, I say to her in as stern a voice as I can muster "if I allow you outside, you must promise me not to go outside of the fence, understand?"

She kind of looks around at the fence with attitude, I can almost hear her saying 'really' but she lowers her head in agreement. Both Jacob and Mattie watch this interaction and neither of them seemed surprised ... but I did see them trying not to laugh.

As we're enjoying Mattie's delicious supper, talking about Hawaii and the wedding, I realize that Mattie hasn't been surprised with any of the strange happenings over the last few days. Sensing my camera calling to me, I say to Jacob and Mattie that we need a picture of the three of us. "Mattie, you're not in any of my pictures."

Getting a gut feeling, I head inside for my camera bag, still at the door, Holding out my hand, nothing happens, but when I touch the bag, instantly it's unzipped and the camera is in my hand. The tri-pod is out of the bag, standing, ready to go. I see Jacob watching. Walking to the door, the camera turns itself on and the dial changes to the setting needed.

Setting up the tri-pod and camera, then pressing the timer button, I run to take my seat between Jacob and Mattie and wait ... No click, no flash, nothing. We all sit there not moving, knowing the moment we do, the camera will go off.

After another minute I get up and walking over to look at the display, without touching the camera, the first picture on the screen is of the three of us, sitting as we were but we're in ancient dress at an old wooden table, silver goblets in our hands. Another picture quickly flashes up, this one of Mattie looking much as she looks now but Jacob is a little boy, again in ancient style clothing. 'Oh my gosh, Jacob as a little boy and Mattie was taking care of him way back then.' Tears spring to my eyes and I can hardly see the next picture. It's the one I just took, well almost, Mattie has the biggest smile on her face, Jacob and I are also smiling, holding hands across the big table ... and we each have a thin band of gold around our heads.

My wedding band now seems to be pulsing on my finger. Taking the camera off the tri-pod, I hand it to Jacob and he looks at it the same time as Mattie, I wondered what they're actually seeing. As the pictures pop up, Jacob and Mattie glance at each other.

I think Jacob's heart must have stopped, I know mine did. Clearing her throat, Mattie sits back in her chair, then proceeds to tell us that her family has been taking care of Jacob's family for hundreds of years. She was assigned to Jacob when he was born, when his mother took him away at a very young age, she could do nothing but have watchers watch him, no interference, no real protection. When he came back with his father, she was there waiting and has been there ever since and she assures us, she will be forever. So now we know, another long time, life time 'friend.'

Relieved, happy, sitting back sipping cold, delicious white wine, looking up at the night sky filled with the same stars we saw in Hawaii ... I think I hear Michael laughing.

Finishing off my wine, I'm standing at poolside when one of my favourite, romantic songs starts playing in my head. Turning, I see Morgan standing there with Jacob. So happy to see him, I run to give him a kiss. "Thank you for singing to me again" I say and he laughs, "I forgot, my wedding gift to you. Any song I have sung to you, you can replay in your head by just thinking about it." "Wow" I say, "so, I didn't expect to see you so soon, can you stay?" I ask him. "Not for long" he answers and goes on to say "we heard about a bit of trouble and I had to make sure for myself." "What! What kind of trouble?" I ask. Leading us to the table, we all sit down.

"Well, no surprise, the news of your wedding spread a little more quickly that we thought it would and the 'enemy' have been spotted." "The Black Knights, the evil ones" he explains. Closing my eyes I try to understand what he just said. "These are the guys that cause accidents that will affect the future, for example, Jacob's little cousin. His death or disability would have affected his life, the life of his family and thus alter their future. Jacob and your gifts are to stop these guys, you are, in effect, the White Knights. Back in time you all would have been very powerful, magically. In the present day, only so much can be done to do or undo these events, again, think of how easy it was for you to save Jacob's cousin. Where we can provide help was by putting the picture where you would see it, figure it out and thus, recognizing the situation and act on it, you were prepared and that is your job, we are here to protect you both, that is our job.

You were safe today because you flew out of another airport. No one, not even me, knew of your last minute change of plans, that actually protected you. When Mattie called me and said you were home, I had to come. Everything is fine now, you guys carry on with your normal routines and try not to worry. Now that you are both aware, you'll recognize any signs more quickly, the signs will come to you, like having pictures on your camera that you know you didn't take. You did an amazing job with the cousin, it was easy for you and you didn't even know what it was all about. Remember, you're a team, you are meant to work together.

It's been a very long day and suddenly I'm feeling very tired.

19

The Pictures

We both agree that it's time to get back to the office. I have a new studio that I haven't seen the inside of for a week and I haven't even downloaded my recent photos so I'll do it at the office. Jacob is taking an awful lot of messages off the answering machine, mostly congratulations, a few about Sam's ex Rick and the guys from the modelling agency want to get together before they all have to get back to work, most in different parts of the country or the world.

Another big change in life, I hadn't realized how fast time was passing. How's that going to work for Jacob ... and more importantly, me? Ready to go, he grabs his briefcase, me my camera bag, we're going to drive together. The sky is a clear blue, no clouds at all but I do see a glint of silver way up there, following it I see a small plane. Until they built the new airport outside of Mara, we never saw planes flying overhead, it's kind of neat wondering who's up there, where they're coming from or where they're going. I hate flying so watching from terra firma is just fine with me.

Our friends at the office are happy to see us back, it takes me 30 minutes to get to my studio. Following me, Elizabeth tells me Dean and her have set a wedding date and she wants all the help I can give her, of course, I'll be taking the wedding photos. Complaining that she missed my wedding, I'm going to download the pictures and she'll be the first to see them. As I requested, a large flat screen has been installed and connected directly to my computer. My plan is to run a slide show of my photographs on the flat screen, instead of just having pictures of my work on the walls, this way, all it will take to change is a click of the mouse, I can't wait.

Plugging my camera into the computer, everything turns on and the photos start to download, enough time for me to run upstairs and get a cup of tea. When I get back, everything is downloaded into my program. Preoccupied with my editing, I don't hear Rick come up behind me, looking at the pictures from Hawaii. "Wow" he says, "with pictures like that, everyone is going to be hiring you." Laughing, I shoot the photos up on the flat screen where they almost look life size and so good, you can almost feel the spray coming off the ocean. Walking right up to it to get a closer look, he says "wow." "I know" I laugh.

"How do you do this?" he asks, unbelief on his face. Casually, with a shrug I say "magic."

"OK" he says and walks away. "Oh" he turns back and drops a folder on my deck "welcome back" he smiles as he saunters down the hall. I spend another hour organizing my photo for easier access from home.

Wondering where Jacob is, I head upstairs, I'm hungry. Jacob's with one of the architects so reaching into his pocket to get the car keys, I ask him how long he's going to be. Glancing at his watch, he says "maybe an hour." "OK, I'll be back by then." Giving him a kiss on the cheek, I leave, swinging my hips as a tease. Picking up my purse from my studio, I was going to leave my camera bag but decide to take it. As I pass the computer screen, pictures start to flash up very quickly. They're of Jacob and a beautiful, tall redhead. they're on a beach looking very cozy together. Sitting down, more photos flash past, faster and faster. "Stop" I say holding my hand up to the monitor but it doesn't stop, it continues on the flat screen, larger than life. I can't stand it. I don't know why this is happening.

"Stop" I shout again and when it doesn't, I open the door and run, passing Jacob in the hallway. With my purse and the car keys in my hand, I head for the parking lot. Walking into my studio, Jacob sees the pictures and standing there, not knowing what to think, Elizabeth walks in. "How is this happening?" he asks her. "I don't know" she answers, holding up the end of the plug, "it's not even plugged in." As he runs out the front door, all he sees are the tail lights of his convertible speeding out of the parking lot.

I don't know where I'm going, the car just seems to be driving itself. Pulling up in front of the art gallery,

Michael of course. As I walk up the stone steps, the door opens and Andre is standing there. "Hello hello" he says smiling at me. "It has been too long" he continues as he takes my arm and closes the door. Touching his hands together, he bows to me, a European tradition I think? "Of course, you are here to see Mr. Michael?" he asks me. Nodding, he leads me to the stairway that goes up to the small, private landing. Again, he bows as I ascend the steps.

As I reach the landing, I can already see the light coming from the picture, like a sunbeam shining through a window. "Hello Michael" I say in answer to his greeting. I always feel loved when I come here, unconditional love from Michael. Laying my purse in the corner with the car keys, I sit on the floor in front of him, cross my legs and close my eyes, basking in the warmth that is there for me.

After a few seconds of sitting in total quiet, my mind goes back to the pictures I saw on the screen in my studio. Michael knows all about the studio and is very proud of me although it is not painting, which I think he would prefer. With Michael, I don't need to speak, he can definitely read my thoughts.

'So what are they supposed to mean? Why are they being shown to me now?' Of course, being a woman, when I see Jacob with another, beautiful woman, how am I supposed to feel? Jealous? Mad? Right now I just want to run away, get out of here, quit, give up, run ...

I think I must have fallen asleep. Michael lets me ramble on and on, answering all my own questions. Opening my eyes, I see Andre placing a cup of tea in front of me on a nice china saucer. Also sitting in front of me is a small gift wrapped box, complete with a tiny ribbon and bow. "Where did this come from" I ask Andre as he backs away from me. "Mail, a few days ago" he answers. "Thanks for the tea" I say and take a sip, looking at the gift. Sipping slowly, enjoying the tea, I'm delaying ...

When I have drained my cup, I gently replace it on the saucer. Picking up the small package I pull off the ribbon and carefully unwrap the paper exposing a blue jewellers box. It's a perfect square, 3" by 3", ½" deep. As I slowly lift the top, inside are two sheets of cotton batten material, laying between the sheets are beautiful diamond and sapphire earrings set in yellow gold, they match the ring that Jacob gave me. Instinctively, I lift out the bottom piece of cotton and laying there is a white card, drawn on with coloured pens. The card is outlined in blue with a little bouquet of flowers drawn in the bottom left corner, Michael's mark. Written in black in the centre of the card are the words 'Some day your prince will come.' Looking up, eyes blurry, I hear the voice in my head saying 'I thought this might be a good time for a reminder.' I can see Michael smiling in his knowing way. "Thank you my love" I whisper. 'Till next time' he whispers back.

Leaning back across the floor, I reach for my old cell phone. When the line is picked up on the first ring, I say "Hi, it's me, I'm ok, I'm with Michael."

Jacob had finished up his work and was coming to get me when I ran out of the office. When he saw the pictures on the flat screen, he knew I must be very upset.

He didn't analyse how or why the pictures were there, he was just worried about me. He had no idea where I would go and called everyone and every place he could think of, Sam, Mattie, my new cell which I had left at home on my desk. He freaked when Mattie answered, telling him where she was. Elizabeth gave him a few suggestions but no luck. For all he knew, I could be on the highway heading down the coast, he really had no idea.

I had never done anything like that before with him but he understood how hurt and upset I would be, knowing how very sensitive I am. He felt so bad and at the same time, realized how lost he would be without me, if I left him.... he wouldn't let his mind go there. So he was unbelievable relieved when he answered his cell and it was me, it felt like the breath of life had been blown back into him, like being revived after having died. He started to think that he needed this jolt to really appreciate me, not take anything for granted.

I was talking very softly into the phone so he had to listen carefully so as not to miss what I was saying and how I was sounding. "I'm sorry for running out like that" I said "and I'm sorry if I worried you." "Where are you" he asked, not sounding mad or bossy, just concerned. "Right now I'm at the art gallery.... but I would like to go down to the beach, that nice restaurant. Are you finished there, can you get a ride and meet me, only if you want to though." "If I want to, you have to be kidding. I'll be there in 10 minutes, ok? I love you... very much" he says, his voice chocking. Smiling with the warm feeling growing inside me, I answer "I love you too" as I jump up and grab my purse. Picking up my tea cup and the gift, I say sincerely "thank you Michael" I am grateful and bowing formally, we're both smiling.

I'm sitting on the sand when Jacob pulls up in Rick's little sports car. I hardly notice him walking barefoot towards me because I'm having an argument with Winston. As Jacob gets closer, the white stallion gets clearer and it doesn't look like I'm talking to myself. Stopping, hands on hips, Jacob starts to laugh. "OK, I'll try" I say to end the conversation. Winston nods a greeting to Jacob and gallops off, slowly disappearing. Sitting on the sand beside me he says "what's up with him?" "He said Gwen and him want to take us riding. I told him I can't ride, that I'm actually afraid of horses. Oh stop" I say as Jacob starts to laugh again. "I know, Winston started to laugh at me as well and I know he's not just any horse." Scooting closer Jacob puts his arm around me.

"Seriously" he says, "I was so worried. From my part, I can't explain how or why those old pictures appeared, I know they must have upset you very much, which is a natural reaction, with women" he adds. "When you ran out and I couldn't find you, I freaked. I admit it, if you ever left me, I don't know what I'd do. This has taught me something though, I think this bad thing had been a good thing for me, I realized how much I love you, need you, want you by my side forever. Anything or anyone before you was nothing, meaningless, I have waited my whole life for you, I knew you were special when I first saw you and everything that has happened since you moved here has been magical, I feel that special bond and everything but now I know I can never, don't want to live without you, I love you, I choose you.

I'm sitting, just staring at him. I've never heard him talk so much before, he's obviously done a lot of thinking. When he's finished, I just smile, I have nothing more to add, I think we have both grown today in a good way, a very good way. He's looking at me now, waiting for me to say something and I don't want to. I feel we have both gotten everything we need to out of this already so instead, I hand him the box. Gingerly taking it from my hands, he looks at me and I nod. When he lifts the lid and sees the earrings, his eyes immediately go to my hand and my ring. Watching his eyes for recognition, when he looks at me questioningly I say "look at the card" Awkwardly he lifts out the two pieces of cotton, careful not to drop the earrings in the sand and leaving it where it was, at the bottom of the box, Jacob reads the card.

Looking very closely, almost as closely as I would, he then looks up at me, a big smile on his face. I smile and nod back to him as he carefully replaces the contents and puts the lid back on. Taking a deep, satisfying breath, he then leans over and gives me a nice kiss. Wrapping my arms around his neck, I pull him down onto the sand, my lips never losing his.

Laughing, happy now we sit up and brush ourselves off. Serious for a minute, he takes my face in his hands. "No doubts, don't ever forget that" he says before pulling me to my feet. Noticing our favourite restaurant, he says "let's go." Picking up my shoes. I glance back at the car, my camera bag and purse locked safely in the trunk.

Jacob sees me checking and turns to look out at the ocean. No sailboats today we're both thinking.

Once again we're sitting outside on the sand, the best of both worlds, having a fabulous restaurant meal and enjoying the great outdoors. Perfect. And it is perfect, both Jacob and I have learned a bit more about ourselves and each other today. I feel I have grown in myself and closer in relationship to him and he feels the same way.

Looking at the earrings again, Jacob asks me how they came to be in my possession. "Andre told me they came by mail a few days ago, he hadn't kept the outside wrapping so doesn't know the return address" I answer Jacob, then go on to tell him that the card is exactly the same as the one Michael gave me years ago. Smiling, he hands them back to me. "They perfectly match the ring" I add.

We're just finishing our delicious meal when we hear the hum of a small plane and looking up, sure enough, one is coming in over the ocean and heading to the airport.

When we get home, the first thing I do is go upstairs to change into something more comfortable. I am happy so all sorts of beautiful, romantic music is playing in my head, I can't help but sing along. Joining Jacob on the veranda, suddenly Morgan appears beside me. "You've both had a tough day" he says, staring out at the ocean. "You, Dawn Elizabeth, were 'chosen' because you are pure of heart. You will see... and act without hesitation. Before you and I'm referring to the girl in those pictures, Jacob wasn't ready. He had to mature, grow up. You bring more out of and put more into him than you can ever imagine. You were hurt very deeply today because you care very deeply, love very deeply. The chest pain and lack of breath is from the heart attack. This may be restored or may not. Remember 'all is as it is meant to be.'"

Morgan smiles at me then slowly disappears. I'm still sitting there looking at the light clouds over the ocean when Jacob speaks to me, I suspect Morgan has spoken to him as well. Picking up the binoculars, I look to the horizon and sure enough a small plane is heading directly for us. As we watch, it flies over so close we can almost see the pilot. I don't like this and think we should contact the airport and ask then to change their landing route, they have the whole desert to come in on. Wouldn't it be interesting if we could hear the pilots talking with the airport tower. How can we do that, I wonder....

20

The Boy and the Boat

Waking up later than usual, still in bed, warm in each other's arms, the phone rings. "Oh, hi sweetheart" Jacob answers. 'Sweetheart! Who can this be?' Handing the phone to me, smiling, he says "it's Sam." "Hi, are you heading home now? Oh, ok. Well, have fun, we'll talk to you later, bye." Replacing the phone on its cradle, I tell Jacob "Sam is meeting a friend for lunch then heading home, she told her Mom she should be home by 5:00." "Well" Jacob says "why don't we head down the coast, there's an flea market an hour or so from here on a fisherman's wharf, lots of fun, different things to see and do ... and we could eat out of newspaper. Should make for some good photos as well, we can take our time. How does that sound baby?" "G R E A T" I shout, jumping up. "Let's go."

We are packed, up and out of there in record time. Wow! A giant flea market, a fisherman's wharf. Sounds like the greatest photo ops ever. Once we hit the coastal road, all there is to look at is the ocean. There are lots of boats on the water, mostly big sailboats all blowing the same way, north at this time of morning. The sky is blue, the sun is shining and I'm happy to say, a little cooler by the water. The heat of Vegas kind of drained me.

The flea market is wonderful ... crowded enough to make it exciting but not overly so. There are many booths and tables offering every possible thing you could dream of. Jacob is carrying my bags, I'm taking pictures of everything. Not really into browsing others peoples' junk, so mostly he just follows close behind me. I like my shadow. He is attracting a lot of attention though but I don't think he minds. My handsome prince. Turning, I put my arms around him, snuggling into his warmth. When he puts him arms around my shoulders, I feel very protected. I like it ...

After two hours of walking around the booths and tables, Jacob now carrying a variety of odds and ends, we decide to stop for lunch. At the end of the wharf there are a few small restaurants set up, complete with bistro tables and umbrellas overlooking the water. The pier is so long you seem to walk forever, further and further out over the ocean. At first you are over sand, where people are walking and playing underneath you, then over shallow water where again, people are playing in the water and swimming, then the pillars go down into the deep water. I imagine sharks circling the pylons.

The wharf is wide, the 'real' fishermen stake out their space with chairs, a table, a cooler for food and cold drinks and another cooler to hold their catch. The have multiple fishing rods spaced along the rail, their hope is to catch whatever is down there. Every fish caught is taken home for dinner. Every so often we would hear shouts as someone got a strike, it's a long way up to the actual wharf from the water so everyone leans over the rail to watch it ascend, twisting and turning, it's a real social thing. I get some great action photos, Jacob is amused by the antics.

There's a outdoor restaurant at the end of the wharf with a few tables and chairs. While Jacob orders a variety off the lunch menu, I walk to the railing with my camera and looking around, I spot an island not far away. Snapping a picture down the length of the wharf, my eyes continue on to the old fashioned boardwalk that leads to a small amusement park. The rides are moving but almost in slow motion. Maybe it's the quiet time between the heat of the day and the cool of the night, I wonder if there are lights on the rides. That would look nice and make for a good picture.

In front of the amusement park is a large yacht club, very expensive looking, full of long sailboats with high masts plus a lot of motor launches, some so big they looked like they could cross the ocean. I never could understand people spending so much money on a boat when most of the time they never leave the dock.

As we're eating, Jacob's cell rings, startling me. Grabbing it, he turns away, a worried look coming over his face. He talks into the phone for a few minutes, gesturing with his hands then he hangs up. He sits there thinking before looking at me. Now I'm worried. "Give me your camera" he instructs me. As I touch it, it turns on. Lifting the strap over my head, I pass it over to him. He scrolls through then stops, then he looks at his watch. It's 5:30. Carefully studying 'the' picture, I know it must be the one of the child. Passing the camera back to me, the boy in the picture is Little Jacob. Oh my goodness!!! The child looks like he is asking a question, permission, a worried look on his little face. There is a mans hand grasping his little arm, but it doesn't look like it's helping him. The boy is standing in water, about 6" of it. What does all this mean?

Jacob tells me that was Sam on the phone. Little Jacob's father showed up shortly after noon and told Sam's mother that he was taking J.J. out for lunch. He said Sam knew about it and he assured her they would be home before Sam. Mom believed him and they left. When Sam got home and they weren't back yet, she got worried. He usually didn't take Little J for that long and Rick wasn't answering his cell. She didn't know what to do next so she called me. Jacob told her to call the police, maybe they could find Rick's vehicle, for starters. For some reason, Jacob immediately thought of the picture.

I'm still staring at the picture of Lil' J when the camera jumps to an earlier picture I took, Jacob is watching over my shoulder. "I took this picture but I don't see any clues in it" I say to Jacob.

"What about that?" he asks pointing to the tiny sailboat in the distance. I did notice that all the boats seemed to be heading north, I figured they went with the wind. Now I see that all but one are heading in the same direction. Good catch Big J.

Zooming in as close as I can on the photo of the boat and the one of Lil' J, the photos are changing slowly, the seconds counting down. Damn ...

Sipping our coffee we sit at a small round table facing the marina. My mind is spinning but as soon as we sit down, the ocean below us, the gulls circling overhead, surrounded by wide blue sky and sunshine, my whole system starts to slow down. Being in nature always does that for me.

Going over the pictures again, they are closer now and sharper, I can definitely see the water getting deeper around Lil' J's feet. As Jacob studies the pictures, I walk over to the railing to scan the boats in the harbour. I'm looking for one that looks similar to the one in the picture. There's a lot of activity going on around the marina. I also notice a Coast Guard office down there.

"Jacob, pass me your cell please." I say to him and hitting Sam's home number, she grabs it on the first ring. Taking a deep breath to calm myself, I'm hoping to calm her, she is freaking out, naturally so, given the circumstances. She assures me she has done what Jacob told her and phoned the police, they are pulling into her driveway as we speak. "Tell them everything you can think of" I say to her "but I have a few questions for you ok?" I hear her hesitate, wondering what ... why... so I quickly jump in "You know how strange, unreal things

always seem to happen around Jacob and me? Well I'll
tell you more later but for now just trust us. We have a
hunch how we might be able to find Lil' J. What I need
to know is did Rick ever own a boat, a sailboat to be
specific?" No sound for a minute or two, I can hear her
mother answering the front door, the sound of voices in
the background.

She's still there and slowly answers "well, he had
an old sailboat years ago. He never actually sailed it,
it just sat in the water. Once in a while he would go
down and pretend to work on it, I think it was just a
place to sit and drink beer." "Where did he dock it? A
club or what?" I ask her, trying to think. Jacob is at my
elbow now, listening, watching and rubbing my arm.
"He did have it in the marina right here but it got so
run down and bad looking, they made him move it out.
I think he took it down the coast somewhere, not too
far because the engine was unreliable, he never really
was a sailor. "Anything special about this boat, any
distinguishing features" I now ask her. "Well, I don't
remember the name of it but it did have an ugly red stripe
along the bow." Ok, now I have something more to go
on. "Thanks Sam, don't worry, Jacob and I have a hunch
and are working on it. Sit tight and we'll stay in touch."

Pulling the small pair of binoculars out of my bag,
I scan the boats in the yacht club. From high atop the
wharf you have a good view but there are so many, it's
impossible to find the one we're looking for.

Telling Jacob my thoughts as I see them, I start by
going over what we know which is: Lil' J is with his
father, he used to own a boat, that boat has a red strip

down the side of it. Looking up at Jacob, I continue "we have pictures in our camera of a boat with a red stripe down its side, we have a picture of Lil' J standing in water, looking worried."

Suddenly feeling a vibration coming from my camera, a new picture pops up in the display, quite tiny and just as one of the restaurant guys is picking up our empty plates. Looking over my shoulder he says "ah, good picture of the amusement park at night with the lights on, lights on in the harbour too." I take another look at the picture, zoom in a bit and see that he is right. The picture must be taken from out on the water. Turning around to see if this is even possible, I look back at the display, the amusement park, the yacht club. It looks very impressive, very expensive.

Passing the camera to Jacob, I walk to the railing again. I don't see any shabby boats here. "OK, here's what I think we should do. Let's walk down to the yacht club office, show them the picture. Maybe they've seen it, maybe it was docked here, they might even have some personal information on the owner." Jacob agrees and getting up, picking up all my bags, he hands me back the camera. Slipping the strap over my head, I grab my purse, it's the least I can carry.

Walking into the yacht club office, I look around for someone who looks like he might be in charge.

Smiling professionally, I beckon one guy over, he looks to be about 60, a military type man. "Hi" I say. "Do you have an office where we can talk in private?" Hesitating, he looks us over, me in my shorts and sleeveless blouse, windblown and sunburned and Jacob, a big hulking man. Yikes, I would be uncertain as well. Taking only a moment to assess us, he turns and leads us into the only office with a door that closes out the public. Indicating the two chairs, after we have put our packages on the floor, we take a seat.

"We need your help" I state dramatically. I figured appealing to his strong man, maiden in distress scenario might bring out his protective side and he would be willing to listen to our story. "OK" he says. Pulling out my camera I say "we're looking for my friends ex who has taken her son. They may be on his boat here in your marina." I see his eyebrow go up. Quickly I continued. "I say 'taken' mildly. He picked up the child around noon, while his mother was out of town. He or the child have not been heard from since, he's not answering his cell. We have reason to believe he has taken the boy to his boat and may be somewhere around here. We also believe the boy is in danger." I say all this with authority because I don't want to show him the pictures and explain that this was my 'authority.' I know he wouldn't understand.

Showing him the best picture we have of the boat, one that I had zoomed in on, for all he knew, I could have taken that picture when we were all friends, enjoying an outing in the boat. He holds my camera and studies the picture closely, more closely than I would have thought. Watching as he punches something into his computer, after reading whatever comes up on the screen, he picks up the phone. Oh oh ... was he calling the police?

A second later, in walks one of the guys I saw at the front counter. "Sir" he says on entering the office. Our man turns the flat screen around so the younger man can read it. "Confirmed Sir. That boat was here earlier. I personally saw it pull out today about 2:30 Sir. Don't imagine it went far, engine didn't sound too good." As this conversation is going on, my mind is thinking ahead to the newest picture. Flipping back to the pic of Lil' J, now the water is up to his waist. Oh my ...

Quickly passing the camera to Jacob, his eyes pop. I'm probably starting to look scared and closing my eyes, I need to think. The last picture was from out on the water, looking back to where we were on the wharf, by the amusement park. What is out there? Standing, I turn and look out through the office window. Focussing my eyes, I see it ... the island. Facing the older man, urgency in my voice now, I'm feeling very military.

"Sir" I say. "We need the Coast Guards' help. I believe that small boy is in the bottom of that sailboat and it is somewhere near or around that island." As I say 'that island', I turn and point out the window. "And the boat is sinking." With those last words, Jacob jumps up. I can see the older man's mind is quickly following what I am saying. As he picks up the phone on his desk, he looks through the window. "We have a problem, get the boat ready, I'll be right there." Marching through the office door he continues on out the front door. As Jacob and I reach down to grab our belongings, the young man signals to Jacob, saying "leave it, I'll watch it for you." We run out the door after the Captain.

The engines on the Coast Guard vessel are revving up, sounding impatient to be going. The four man coast guard crew are waiting for us at the foot of the ramp. Jacob jumps on board behind the Captain as the guys help me on. The two older men exchange greetings. saluting one another. Nice. The three younger guys are preparing the boat, one is already steering us out of the harbour. A minute later, we are flying over the water, the spray hitting me in the face, I can just feel my hair curling up.

"OK young lady, what is the story?" the captain of the boat asks me once we have steadied out. I tell him the story from the start and that I believe we will find the boat, with the boy in the cabin, somewhere around this island. It's only a 15 minute ride in this boat but in a broken down old one, it would take a lot longer. As we're getting closer to the island, it's getting dark. Great! Nothing like having a fear of water and now it's dark so ... fear on dark water. Turning to look back towards the shore, now with the lights starting to come on, it looks exactly like the picture on Cam.

Trying to get an exact fix of where on the island this angle would have been taken from, we troll a short distance as tight to the east side of the island as we can. Ten minutes later, we find it, half hidden behind a huge fallen tree ... and sinking. As they pull the Coast Guard boat in as close as is safe, Jacob and I are standing at the side, I think I'm going to throw up. The broken boat looks so scary, lopsided in the black water. My gosh ... if Lil' J is in there, he'll be scared to death.

Tears starting to sting my eyes, I can't stop myself any longer. Standing beside me, I sink my head into Jacobs' chest. "Hey Little J.... are you there? Can you hear me? It's Jacob and Donna. We've come to get you and bring you home" Jacob is calling out towards the boat, I can hardly speak now. Feeling Jacob's hand tighten on my arm, I felt so bad for him, I know how much he loves that little boy.

While we watch, two of the coast guards climb on board, balancing themselves on the wobbling deck. Inching towards the cabin door, we hear it, a tiny little cry. Eyes wide open, Jacob and I look at each other then watch as the men pull a little boy up out of the opening, dripping wet up to his armpits. Neither of us could really see him clearly through the flood of tears that were pouring out of our eyes but we could see the pure joy on the faces of each and every man on that boat. They knew they had done a good thing tonight and saved that little boy's life.

When Little J is handed over to the men on board, Jacob pulls him into his big arms and hugs the breath out of him. He is freezing, having been in that cold water for hours. Handing us warm blankets, Jacob wraps the little body in one and curls up in a windless corner of the boat, tucking Lil' J in his arms. I can't wait to see the pictures on Cam.

Before we pull away from the sinking boat, the men check the inside as well as the water around the boat. I catch them giving each other a strange look but they carry on so ... Hmm.... It took the ride back to the marina for my heartbeat to regulate itself and the tears to stop flowing. Sitting curled up beside Jacob, my head in my hands, the first thing we need to do is phone Sam, give her the good news. She will probably have to speak to the authorities, she is the only one who can explain our involvement in this. Hopefully, we won't be kept here very long. Suddenly I am very tired and looking over at the J's ... they're both asleep.

When we get back to the marina, Jacob and I both personally thank each man who was on board and took part in this rescue. I give each of them a hug and a kiss then take a picture of them standing in front of their Coast Guard boat. Telling them they are real heroes, what they did tonight would never be forgotten, their story would go down through generations of this young boys families. Waving to them from the ramp, they all have big smiles on their faces. I feel something special is going to happen to these guys in the near future.

Walking into the same office we were in earlier, Lil' J is fast asleep in Jacob's strong arms. Our packages are exactly where we left them, safe and sound.

Picking up Cam, I turn her on. The first picture is of the restaurant on the sand except there is a different boat on the water, the photo of all the boats heading north... is gone. The photo of the wharf, the amusement park and the marina with all its light on is still there, it looks beautiful and unique, the lights sparkling.

This time the yacht club office and coast guard office are also lit from inside and you can almost make out the guys inside. A nice keepsake. The one of Lil' J, now he's standing in his swimming trunks, very colourful, at the edge of our pool, squinting up at us, a big smile on his face. The date on the corner of this last picture is one week from today. Looking up, I see Jacob quietly watching me. Taking a big breath then breaking into a smile, he smiles too, everything is alright. 'I love you' I mouth to him. "I love you too" he says softly.

There is one more picture, very dark water. I can't quite make out what it is.

I don't know how long we were asleep in the office chairs before we hear someone walk in and put cups down on the desk. A smiling Captain informs us that "phone calls have been made to Sam, we've spoken to the police at that end, you are free to leave ... with our heartfelt thanks."

Continuing on with a soft smile, the Captain tells us that Sam burst into tears hearing that her son was ok. He gave her a brief summary of what had taken place saying he was sure we would give her the full report. When she asked to speak to us, she was told all three of us were asleep in his office. Knowing that everyone was ok, she would wait for us to call her.

Drinking our coffee to wake us up for the drive home, we chat with the Captain for a few minutes while one of his men gets our car, kindly loading my purchases in the back. Standing, we tell him we're going to hit the highway and head straight for home. Shaking his head, he tells us that he has never seen anything like this in his 45 years in the military. Laughing, I tell him the boy obviously has a guardian angel watching over him. We all smile. We thank him and his men again for believing us and for their quick response. They are all heroes today. As we're belting Lil' J into the back seat, I noticed spotlights on the water, around where we found the boat. I wonder what's going on over there?

Tucked up and belted into the back seat, Lil' J is fast asleep, Jacob and I are now starting to wake up. It's midnight and we have a two hour drive ahead of us.

"Are you ok to drive?" I ask Jacob, saying he is a bit tired, but anxious to get home. Smiling over at me, he says "we'll stop and pick up a coffee for the road, maybe even a donut or two." As we pull out of the marina, heading straight towards the inland highway, flatter, straighter and faster, I pull Jacob's cell out of his pocket and punching in our home number, Mattie grabs it on the second ring. "Everyone ok?" are the first words out of her mouth, as if she had an inside scoop on today's happenings ... and it didn't sound as if I had woken her up. Hmmm ...

"Mattie, I'd like to invite Sam and her mother to come and stay the night. I think we would all feel better doing this. Would you mind making up the spare rooms for them, we can talk about all this tomorrow. "No problem lady" she tries to sound mad and laughing I say "see you in a couple of hours." Jacob is nodding his head up and down at me and smiling. I think the seriousness of this adventure is starting to sink in to us. I don't know what I would do if anything happened to Jacob. Leaning across the seat, I steal a quick kiss, he kisses me back.

Now I punch in Sam's number, she grabs it on the first ring, she knows it is us. "Hi sweetheart" Jacob yells across the car as I start to talk to Sam. I shoot him daggers and mouth 'sweetheart' then smile and turn back to the cell. "Sam, I want you and your mother to head over to our place, plan on staying the night. No, nothing is wrong. We just think it might be nice for all of us to be together. We can talk about everything tomorrow. Mattie is expecting you and we should be home in about 2 hours. Yeah, he's fast asleep on the back seat. Ok, see you soon." "Bye" Jacob again calls out.

Relief is sinking in on him now and he is wired. We are flying down the highway, no cop cars in sight. Hmmm.... we did tell them we would be taking the inland highway. Looking upwards I quietly whisper "thank you Lord," not just for the highway, but for the entire day ... and I do still have a trunk full of treasurers from the flea market. That now seems so far away, we'll have to come back and bring Sam. Wow! I am amazed at how fast I can get over something like this. Is that a good thing? Maybe so ...

Laying my head on Jacob's shoulder, I'm not tired but need to feel his warmth, I cannot wait to get into bed beside him tonight, after a day like this. Suddenly I get the urge to turn the stereo on and guess who's singing ... you guessed it, our friend Morgan is crooning one of our favourite love songs. Snuggling into Jacob's shoulder, I can feel him smiling. "You know" I say "I get the feeling we are never alone anymore." Looking down at me he nods. Lucky us, actually.

As we pull into our driveway, the front doors fly open, the light from within shining out into the darkness, making me wonder once again about the goings on around the sinking boat.

Jumping out, I grab my camera bag as Jacob unbuckles and picks up Lil' J. Striding to the front door, Sam, Mattie and Sams' mother are waiting anxiously. Sam is hopping up and down, smiling but with tears running down her face. Mattie is standing with her arm around Sams' Mom, both women are also crying. Jacob walks right past the ladies, straight into the kitchen and lays Lil' J on the loveseat in the corner. Hands are pulling at him, Lil' J is being smothered by Sam and her mom. Having handed over his responsibility, Jacob backs away as Mattie, wrapping her arms around him, looks up and says knowingly "job well done."

Standing back, just watching, I hear a click from inside my camera bag. As I reach for it, the camera is in my hand, turned on and showing me a picture of three happy faces. The direction is from where I am now standing, pointing towards the loveseat but in the photo, Sam and Mom are on either side of Lil' J, they are all posing for me and smiling. The sun is shining in through the windows. Tomorrow is going to be a very happy day I predict.

Little J promptly lays back on the loveseat and falls asleep, Sam picks him up and heads down to the spare room. Her Mom stands up at the same time, saying she is also very tired and is ready for bed. As she passes Jacob, who is perched on a stool by the island, she stops, puts her arms around him and whispered very close to his ear "thank you for saving my grandson." Jacob had to lean down to hear her soft voice, he didn't say a word, just nodded humbly.

Coming back into the kitchen, Sam helps herself to a glass of wine. As expected, Mattie has prepared a light snack, I'm starving. We had last eaten nine hours ago. There is something to be said about eating with your eyes closed, I think we're all feeling the same, totally exhausted. "So how did you know?" Sam almost sounds likes she's afraid to ask the question. My eyes pop open and I look at Jacob, who's looking at me. Mattie is watching us both, waiting.

"Why don't we talk about this tomorrow, when we are more awake" she suggests. My mind is thinking 'where do we start ... and what exactly do we tell her.' I decide I need wine. "Let's just say that Lil' J has a guardian angel watching over him." When I say that, Jacob gave me kind of a sarcastic look. What? I take a sip of wine, waiting for someone else to say something, Jacob or Mattie, anybody but no one does. Why is it up to me? OK. Jacob has known Sam for years and I have only known her for a few months but I feel like I have known her for years. She is just that really nice, normal type of person, we've spent a lot of time together and I like her. She would do anything for us, I feel that. So ... how much do I tell her?

While my mind is racing through all these thoughts, she says "I know there is something special about you two. I've seen some strange things but I have a feeling it's all good, nothing scary. I trust you guys in ... everything." Jacob looks over at me, almost begging me to tell her. I look over to Mattie and lowering her eyes, she nods. Well, ok then. "OK Sam" I say, "Jacob and I are connected ... spiritually, from way back in time. Some other friends are also." I've decided I'm not going to tell her anything I don't need to. "We have our own guardian angels watching over us and sometimes directing and guiding us to help others in trouble. That seems to be our job right now. It was explained to us by a 'friend,' that we would save or rescue or stop bad things from happening to people and especially children, things that would affect their future lives and the lives of others around them." I stop and wait, Sam is thinking. I take a sip of wine. Jacob and Mattie are also listening to my explanation.

Suddenly, I realized Sam needs to know what exactly happened today from the time she called us to say Lil' J was gone. While waiting she went over the situation with her ex-husband and after our talk, a calm came over her and she just sat back, knowing we were on it and everything would be ok.

She didn't know how she knew, she just knew. And now she just needed to know how she knew. She would forget the details of our story, her mind would be at ease and they would all be able to go on with life, under a positive note, this incident literally forgotten. A bad memory. I remember Morgan explaining it to me.

"You and Jacob are given these gifts so that lives will go on as they were meant to. Evil will not win." Sam was now looking at me to continue. Looking for my camera, as my eyes see it, my hand reaches out and it jumps into my hand and turns on. Sam sees this, her eyes popping open. The picture on the screen is the one of Lil' J laughing up at us by the edge of our pool, he's ready to go swimming. Passing the camera over to Sam, when she sees the picture of her son, she smiles then looks up at me questioning.

"A picture similar to this one appeared on my camera all by itself about three days ago. In the picture was a little blond child, not clear so we couldn't tell who it was, the child was not smiling, he was looking up, concerned. There were two inches of water around his shoes. The date on the camera, at the time, was three days ahead. We had a few other pictures on the camera. Jacob and I know by now to keep checking these pictures and today, the one of Lil' J came into focus, as the day went on, the water got deeper and deeper.

We also had a few pictures of a white sailboat with a red stripe down the bow." Sam was listening carefully now, trying to understanding. "So that's why you were asking me about Rick's old boat" she whispers, almost to herself. "The picture of the boat also got clearer and clearer. When you called us, we were on the wharf. The last picture to appear was of the wharf at night with the lights on and the amusement park next to it. The picture was taken from the island. That was the spot where we found the boat, half sunk, with Lil' J down below in the cabin. When the Coast Guard pulled him up, he was dripping wet up to his arm pits" I dramatized. No one said a word. We all got the picture.

I took another big sip of wine, so did Jacob and Mattie. Sam just stared into space. I could see the true reality of it coming to her now and she was just starting to choke when I put out my hand to touch her shoulder. She stopped and looked up at me. "Good has triumphed over evil today. This is the way it should be. Don't think about what 'might have happened,' it didn't. Rejoice" and laughing, I stand up and hold my glass high. I'm starting to feel the wine now but everyone else stands up laughing, holding up their glass.

"All is well" I say and to echos of the same, crystal clinks and wine is drunk. Still laughing, we pull our stools in closer to the food and dig in ... It's then that

Mattie goes to the fridge and pulls out a layer of our beautiful wedding cake. Hmmm, how appropriate I think ... another occasion to celebrate. While I'm accepting a piece of cake from Mattie, I hear Morgan's voice in my head ... he's singing one of my favourite songs. Silently, I hold up my glass ... 'to special friends.'

We're still in bed at eleven the next morning having only gone to bed at five am. I can hear the sound of splashing in the pool but it's the ringing of the phone that really wakes me up.

A little tap on the door and Mattie walks in, the phone in her hand. Jacob is dead to the world so she passes the phone to me. "Hi, this is Dawn" I say, "Oh, hello Captain, fine thank you. Ok, tell me. Thank you captain, I'll get Sam for you, hold on a second." Jacob is now sitting up in bed, looking over at him I say quietly "they found Ricks' body in the water beside the boat last night. That was the lights we saw. They believe he fell on the deck, hit his head and rolled into the water. He will be autopsies before they can release cause of death. The Captain wants to personally notify Sam." Walking out to the patio where Sam is sitting, Lil' J is in the water, Jacob sits down beside her and hands her the phone.

Walking downstairs, Jacob is at the bottom of the stairs wearing only boxer shorts. He looks pretty hot. Pulling him in close to me, nice and warm, I ask "where do you thing you're going dressed like that?" Kissing him on the lips, he kisses back then ... "Oh, hi Winston." Jacob spins around to see a ghostly vision of Winston standing right there in our hallway. We wait and he just stands there, also waiting. The only feeling I get is that we will be seeing him again. Maybe Winston is in place of a picture. As he disappears, I take Jacob by the hand and lead him back to the bedroom.

Laying down together on the bed we start really kissing, the best ever ... for about two minutes, then we both lay back on our pillows, arms splayed. What now I wonder aloud. "I imagine Sam will go home after lunch" Jacob says hearing Mattie and then Sam calling J.J. out of the pool.

As we sit down around the kitchen table, which is again laden with food, I ask Sam how she is. "OK" she says, looking a bit sad. To get her to talk it out, I ask about Rick. Her and I have never talked about him, Jacob did fill me in a bit when I first met J.J., so she tells me of how she and Rick dated then lived together for about two years. She felt a strong urge to have a child and really had to talk him into it. Because he was so reluctant to become involved or take any responsibility, when she got pregnant, they signed a legal document that J.J. was hers solely and she would not expect or ask anything of him, ever. Every few years Rick dropped in to see J.J. but that was it. There was nothing romantic between Sam and him and J.J. didn't know that he was his father, so there is nothing to miss.

She does know that J.J. is the beneficiary of Rick's life insurance, he told her that last year, now she just feels sad for a life ended. Offering her any help she might want or need we assure her we will attend the funeral with her. As we're eating an exceptional lunch that Mattie has served, Sam says she plans on heading home shortly. She also tells us that her mother will be moving in with her, they've been talking about this for almost a year now. She's getting older and Sam would like her closer, J.J. will be starting school in a month and with her mother living with them, he'll be able to attend a local private school, a win-win situation for all of them. They're all very happy about this plan. "And" I quickly add in, "your Mom and Mattie can get together more often." I say this because I see Mattie and Sams' Mom seem to get along very well.

As Sam and her Mom are packing the car, I wander downstairs and see J.J. playing with my keyboard, the same one that I haven't touched for months. "Play something for me" he begs. "Well, ok, what?" Picking up the music book from the stand, he hands it to me. "Play this one."

I used to know this one so give it a shot, J.J. just sits in awe, listening to me. Towards the end, he is sort of humming along. I think he has a good sense of rhythm. When we turn around, Jacob and Sam are standing in the doorway, smiling. "Ready to go?" Sam asks her son, holding out her hand. Walking them out to the car, after goodbye hugs and kisses and a 'see you soon,' they drive off.

It's nice to be home and alone at last. I need to plug into my house and renew myself. With our arms around each other, we walk in the front door and as Jacob detours into his office, I walk down the hall into the kitchen ... and stop in my tracks. The entire kitchen is cleared up and I catch Mattie waving her hand towards the fridge as the food floats into it. She knows I am behind her and slowly, dramatically turns around to

Truly

look at me, her arm still in the air. I'm standing there with my hands on my hips.

"Well?" I say to her. Pulling up a stool at the island, I do the same. At that moment Jacob walks into the room, glancing from one of us to the other, he says "what's up?" and leans against the wall. I know him, if the conversation gets boring, he will slip away. I hesitate a moment then jump up and head for the stove, I feel like a cup of tea.

Suddenly in front of my place sits a cup of tea. Mattie is smiling. Jacob is sitting down now. The tea is perfect and now Mattie turns to Jacob and asks if he would like anything. He doesn't speak but another cup of tea appears in front of him. Now we are both staring at her. "OK" I say. "It's like this" she says. "Have you noticed that your challenges are getting more difficult?" 'Not really' I think. "Well they are and the more difficult, the more your powers are coming out. Did you notice today when you looked for your camera, it zoomed right to you. That's new. Do you notice that you and Jacob can almost read each others minds?" 'Sometimes' I think. Isn't that just part of being a couple. "No" she answers. Hey wait a minute. I haven't said a word and she's answering me. "That's one of my powers" again she answers my thoughts.

"Do you read everything I think?" I glare at her. "Only what you allow me" she answers. Same for you and Jacob. There are lots of things you don't hear. Only when it is relative or an emergency. The more you practice, the better you get. The more you need these gifts, they will be there for you.

"What are your gifts Mattie" I ask her. Well, I have powers that are relative to what I am and do. I only have to think of certain food and baking and it appears. I know you're always amazed at how I have so much perfect food in the house. No matter what time, how many people are here, I always lay out a big spread. Now you know. You just have to think of something you want to eat, I sense it and open the fridge or oven and there you have it. "I am the world's best hostess and I never have to go to the grocery store" she laughs. I wonder if I have that power. What would I like right now?

Ahhh a piece of chocolate layer cake with vanilla ice cream appears before me. I look up at her, eyes wide. She laughs "not you, me." Well, this is a good thing. If I could have anything my little heart desired, I would be eating all day.

Jacob is sitting, chin in his hand, elbow on the table, amusement on his face, just watching both of us. I start to question her more but she holds up her hand and says "you'll know all in good time." "OK, so where is Tabitha? I haven't seen her since we got home last night or early this morning." "She's out there on the diving board, fast asleep." I turn to look out the glass doors and sure enough, there she is. What is she doing there and where has she been all this time. She usually comes running to me when I walk through the door. "Well" says Mattie, "there's something you probably should know about her. She is the one who has kept me informed of what has been happening with you, Jacob and J.J. I've had to keep her in my room and tell her she cannot go to you. We don't want her jumping when we don't know what she is getting into. She is tapped into you, she gave me a play by play since you were on the wharf and started following the pictures. She was so happy when little J.J. was pulled to safety and has stuck to him like glue since the minute he walked in the door. She's on the diving board now because she was watching him swim. Now that her protection job is over, for now, she is exhausted and will probably sleep for hours."

I'm listening to her with my mouth open, this is unreal. She continues "because you are emotionally involved, you will be extremely exhausted afterwards, did you notice that? It will get easier." Hey, did I tell her aloud or think it. Oh oh, Jacob is watching me. Is he reading my mind? This sucks. Taking a sip of tea, it's cold now but still good, my ice cream is all melted, then I see Tabitha out of the corner of my eye, standing at the glass patio doors, looking in at me. Lifting up my hand, I point to the door and flick my wrist, the latch clicks, the door slides open. Tabitha prances in, runs over to me and bounces up on my lap. No problem here I think. Oh wait, she can read my thoughts also. Yikes. Everyone laughs.

I need a shower and I'm dying to download my pictures to the computer. Looking over at Jacob, who's looking very tired, I stand up, take his hand and lead him upstairs. Over my shoulder, I see Mattie point to her apartment door and it opens. Tabitha hops off the stool and runs into the apartment.

Jacob and I get in the shower together, we're both beat. Sudzing each other up, we wash our hair, rinse off then wrap ourselves in king size bath towels before flopping down on the bed. The sun is shining in, nice and warm. Before we know it, we are fast asleep.

I wake up about 6:00 pm and am still tired. Jet lag I think from the wicked last five days. That's ok with me, I know when to take it lazy and this is it. In slow motion I slide off the bed and crawl across the thick carpeted floor to my computer. Sitting crossed legged, I punch the button on the tower and reach up to turn on the screen.

Seeing that my camera bag is not where I usually put it by my desk, I close my eyes trying to remember where I last saw it. Feeling something hit my arm, I open my eyes and there it is. Wow! I kinda like this. While the computer is booting up, I take out the camera and turn it on. Still half asleep, this carpet is so nice, extra thick and soft, I want to be a baby and just crawl around.

Laying on my back, holding the camera over my head, I scroll through. Seeing all the magic in the pictures. I want to print out some enlargements and put them on the walls of my studio, now that would be good advertising. Unable to hold my arms up any longer, before I know it, I'm asleep on the floor.

Eyes snapping open to a sound I haven't heard in the bedroom before, a TV, to be precise, a very large, flat screen TV mounted on the wall just above me, just came on. Where are my cork picture frames that were there? Hearing the channels changing, I sit up to see Jacob laying in bed, still in his towel, like I am and holding the remote. "Cable" I ask. "Satellite" he replies. Yeah! "Hundreds of channels" I shout as I jump on the bed and reach for the remote. He is fast and quickly tucks it under the covers. Ha! Where did this come from and why didn't I notice it before. "It's my wedding present to you" Jacob says.

"I wanted to surprise you. I know you like to watch while you're working on your pictures and computer, so I thought of this" he smiles as he says this, very proud of himself. Wow. 'I'm very proud of you too' I think as I lean in and give him a big kiss... and hold out my hand. Laughing, he hands me the remote. Hey, I haven't said a word!!! Now he laughs out loud and says "if we are addressing each other, we can read those thoughts, like just now. I do find sometimes I start to get something from you and think you're talking to me but then it stops. I'm guessing you are actually talking to yourself so it cuts me off. Good idea I think. He laughs.

Oh my gosh.... now I'm afraid to think. "Don't worry" he assures me. One of my favourite shows is just starting so it must be after 7:00 pm. I don't know why I think this as I haven't watched tv in months. Jacob doesn't watch tv with such beautiful weather, why stay indoors. We have watched a couple of movies though. Looking over at him, asking if he wants to watch this show, he nods yes so we snuggle in. After this, I think we need to eat something, he agrees.

"Thanks" I turn to him planting another kiss on his cheek. "It's perfect, scary thought but you really know me. I really need to hear you talk more" I add. He looks at me questioningly. "You rarely say anything, I don't know what you're thinking, how you're feeling about anything, like what happened yesterday. How are you handling this?" He looks at me through his eyelashes,

trying to look strict, then he smiles "just read my mind."
OK, this just might work out, for me that is.

The credits are rolling up as the show we were
watching comes to an end. Glancing out our glass
bedroom wall, I see dark thunderclouds rolling in from
the ocean. This is something I haven't seen yet, I love a
good storm.

Walking to the patio doors, I open them and step
onto our new veranda, standing with his arms around
me, we watch the sky. The rolling thunder is still far out
over the ocean but we hear another sound. Looking up,
a small, private plane is flying through the black clouds.
It goes right over our heads heading towards the airport,
a new one just built, out on the desert.

Throwing on our bathrobes we walk, hand in hand
down to the kitchen to get a late bite to eat. As usual,
Mattie is there, pulling food out of the fridge and setting
up the island. I am not wondering how she always seems
to be at the right place at the right time anymore. Now
that I know, it kind of takes the charm out of it but
I'm happy she's there for us. And here comes Tabitha,
prancing across the counter and literally flying onto me,
tongue going a mile a minute.

Printed in the United States
By Bookmasters